"You think I'm on t

"I know you graduated the same year as the other women."

"The three murders could be completely unrelated—a coincidence."

"And the petals?"

"The petals." The terror from this morning when she'd seen the rose petals on her porch punched her in the gut. She sagged.

"Let's get out of here." Colin peeled her fingers from the gate and laced his own with hers.

They skirted the lingering knots of people in the street, and Michelle tugged on his hand. "So which is it, Colin? Do you believe the killer scattered those petals on my porch or do you believe some innocent bystander carried them there on the bottom of his shoes?"

Colin wanted to reassure her, drive the fear from her big brown eyes, but he couldn't lie to this woman. He couldn't pretend that she didn't face some danger from this wily killer.

"If it's the former, I'll make sure he never gets that close to you again." He tightened his grip on her hand.

CAROL ERICSON

OBSESSION

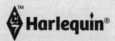

TORONTO NEW YORK LONDON
AMSTERDAM PARIS SYDNEY HAMBURG
STOCKHOLM ATHENS TOKYO MILAN MADRID
PRAGUE WARSAW BUDAPEST AUCKLAND

For my dad, who loved the central coast of California.

Recycling programs
for this product may
not exist in your area.

ISBN-13: 978-0-373-69616-1

OBSESSION

Copyright © 2012 by Carol Ericson

All rights reserved. Except for use in any review, the reproduction or utilization of this work in whole or in part in any form by any electronic, mechanical or other means, now known or hereafter invented, including xerography, photocopying and recording, or in any information storage or retrieval system, is forbidden without the written permission of the publisher, Harlequin Enterprises Limited, 225 Duncan Mill Road, Don Mills, Ontario, Canada M3B 3K9.

This is a work of fiction. Names, characters, places and incidents are either the product of the author's imagination or are used fictitiously, and any resemblance to actual persons, living or dead, business establishments, events or locales is entirely coincidental.

This edition published by arrangement with Harlequin Books S.A.

For questions and comments about the quality of this book please contact us at Customer_eCare@Harlequin.ca.

® and TM are trademarks of the publisher. Trademarks indicated with ® are registered in the United States Patent and Trademark Office, the Canadian Trade Marks Office and in other countries.

www.Harlequin.com

Printed in U.S.A.

ABOUT THE AUTHOR

Carol Ericson lives with her husband and two sons in Southern California, home of state-of-the-art cosmetic surgery, wild freeway chases, palm trees bending in the Santa Ana winds and a million amazing stories. These stories, along with hordes of virile men and feisty women, clamor for release from Carol's head. It makes for some interesting headaches until she sets them free to fulfill their destinies and her readers' fantasies. To find out more about Carol, her books and her strange headaches, please visit her website, www.carolericson.com, "where romance flirts with danger."

Books by Carol Ericson

HARLEQUIN INTRIGUE

*Brothers in Arms
**Guardians of Coral Cove

CAST OF CHARACTERS

Colin Roarke—War hero turned FBI agent, he follows a link between two murdered women that leads him to his hometown, Coral Cove, but he never expects his investigation to endanger the girl next door. But once it does, he'll do anything to keep her safe.

Michelle Girard—Threatened by a killer, she decides to fight back with the help of sexy hometown hero, Colin Roarke. But as the killer's obsession grows more dangerous, she needs more than Colin's help; she needs his protection.

Amanda Stewart—Is she the killer's first victim or just one in a long line until he reaches his ultimate goal?

Alec Wright—A computer geek who teaches at the high school, he has a crush on Michelle and is more than a little jealous that she seems to have found someone else's shoulder to lean on.

Larry Brunswick—Michelle was this math teacher's favorite student; now he's her mentor. Does his interest in Michelle go beyond the classroom?

Chris Jeffers—This transient was caught hiding out in Columbella House after the first murder, and the cops are anxious to pin the crime on him. Do they have their man, or are they jumping the gun?

Bob and Mary Beth Hastings—This couple has a grudge against Michelle because her mother seduced their teenage son. The time just might be ripe for payback.

Nick Schaeffer—A student in Michelle's algebra class, this teen was caught playing some nasty pranks. Did he graduate to something more serious?

Mayor Tyler Davis—He's all about projecting a pristine image of Coral Cove to attract tourists, and a serial killer doesn't fall in line with his plans.

Chapter One

No, I do not need a lifetime supply of Viagra. Michelle Girard snorted as she deleted the unopened email, sending it to the black hole of cyberspace. Maybe Alec Wright, the computer teacher at school, could suggest a better spam filter, one that didn't allow this garbage to slip through to her in-box.

As her cursor hovered over the next message, a breath of apprehension puffed against the nape of her neck and her hand trembled. The words in the subject line punched her in the gut. *Like mother, like daughter?*

Different unknown sender from last month, same message. And just like last month, she deleted the email without opening it or reading it and then cleared her delete folder. She didn't know if the message contained more content than the insidious question, and she didn't want to find out.

She jumped at the sharp rap on her front door and slammed her laptop shut, as if that could banish the disturbing email from her mind. She dropped the math quizzes she had to grade on top of the computer and crept to the door. Twitching back the curtain on the window, she blew out a deep breath and waved at Amanda, her best friend.

Amanda banged on the door and yelled, "Don't just stand there gawking. Let me in, already."

Michelle swung open the door, and Amanda charged

across the threshold, gripping her upper arms, a sweater draped around her shoulders. She gave an exaggerated shiver. "This June gloom sucks."

Michelle peered outside at the once-sunny day now shrouded in a slow-moving fog rolling in from the beach. June days in the little coastal town of Coral Cove usually started out overcast and ended that way.

She snapped the door shut and turned to survey her friend. "What are you doing here, and why are you all dressed up?"

"This old thing?" Amanda glanced down at her shimmering summer dress and plucked at the floral skirt as her sweater slipped to the floor.

"Since you usually work at home in sweats and a T-shirt, there must be some special occasion." Michelle crossed her arms, waiting for news of Amanda's next harebrained scheme. She adored her friend, but she was as flighty as a butterfly in a gust of wind.

"You have to point that out, don't you?" She adjusted the bodice of her dress and spread her arms out, pausing theatrically. "Colin Roarke is back in town."

Michelle raised one brow. "Colin Roarke?"

"Oh, please. Even you with your bookish ways and band of nerds must've heard of the Roarke brothers in high school." She tousled her blond-streaked hair and took a twirl around the room. "Colin was four years ahead of us and Kieran was six years ahead."

"Of course I've heard of them." Michelle dipped to scoop up Amanda's sweater from the floor, her hair sweeping across her suddenly flushed cheeks. She hadn't given Colin Roarke much thought since she'd had a mad, useless, crazy crush on him in high school.

"I know they both got football scholarships to college. The family lived down the road from here." Michelle tilted her head. "Didn't the parents retire to Hawaii or something?

The dad made a killing in the dot-com industry and pulled out before it all went bust."

Amanda's mouth hung open. "Who cares about their parents? Colin is back in town, and he's hotter and hunkier than ever, or so I've heard. I haven't had a peek at him yet, but we're about to remedy that."

"You're going to check out Colin Roarke?" Michelle laughed. Amanda and her husband had separated exactly two months ago, and she spent all her time trying to make him jealous.

"And you're coming with me, so I don't look too obvious."

Michelle smirked. "Yeah, wouldn't want to look too obvious. Where is this rare specimen of hunky manhood and what's he doing back in town? We're the ones with the ten-year reunion this summer."

Amanda formed a pout with her lipsticked mouth. "Too bad Colin wasn't in our class. Maybe I could've snagged him instead of that loser Ryan."

Michelle clicked her tongue feeling like a schoolmarm. "Ryan is not a loser. He's a good cop and he loves you."

"He cheated on me."

"Not exactly. He sent some inappropriate emails to a woman in another state." Michelle's gaze darted to her closed-up laptop. Those inappropriate emails *seemed to be contagious.*

Amanda brushed her hands together. "Whatever. Are you coming with me or not? Colin's at Burgers and Brews, but we'll miss him if you dawdle."

"Early dinner?" Michelle dropped Amanda's sweater across the arm of a chair and checked her watch.

She really had to get those quizzes graded so she could enjoy the rest of her weekend, but she welcomed Amanda's interruption. That email, the second in two months, had spooked her, and she didn't relish the thought of hunkering down in her beach cottage alone as the fog pressed in on her.

"Sure. That's a good excuse." Amanda grabbed Michelle's purse from the table by the window and tossed it to her.

A short drive later in Amanda's Mercedes, they rolled into the center of town. Michelle rubbed a circle in the condensation on the window and peered outside. "You can actually see more than ten feet in front of you here, but that's not going to last long. The fog's on its way."

"And I'm on my way to meet Colin." Amanda threw her car into Park and cut the engine.

Michelle struggled into her sweater as she climbed from the car. "You never did tell me what he's doing back in town. Visiting old friends?"

"That's what he's doing at Bryan's restaurant." Hunching forward, Amanda dabbed at her lipstick in the side mirror. "He was good friends with Bryan Sotelo, but I think he's here on a case."

"A case?" Michelle hugged the sweater around her body against the cool, moist air seeping into her skin. From the town grapevine, she'd heard that Colin had become an FBI agent after returning from Afghanistan to a hero's welcome. There had been some tragedy over there involving his older brother.

"Something about Tiffany Gunderson's accident."

Michelle wrinkled her nose. "The FBI doesn't investigate accidents. She fell down an elevator shaft and broke her neck. It didn't even happen here in Coral Cove. Do they suspect foul play?"

"How am I supposed to know that? You sound exactly like my husband." Amanda grabbed Michelle's arm. "Let's go before Colin leaves."

"Hi, Ms. Girard."

Michelle turned toward the two voices, the greeting

spoken in unison. Four of her students lounged on the bench outside the local pizza place. The two girls waved, their long, skinny legs encased in short shorts and furry boots. The two boys perched on the arms of the bench, their hoods pulled up over their heads, matching teenaged smirks on their faces.

Michelle's heart lurched for a moment before she waved and pasted on a smile. "Enjoy your weekend."

Could one of her students be behind the annoying emails? They probably wouldn't know her history, but their parents might. She hadn't thought of reporting the emails to the police, but a third one might constitute harassment.

Amanda sighed. "Sorry. I forgot it was dollar night at Vinnie's, and some of your snot-nosed students would be hanging around. Just didn't think they'd be here this early."

"Sydney and Maddie are nice girls. I don't mind running into my students as long as I'm not doing something stupid."

"You never do anything stupid, Michelle. Remember dollar nights at Vinnie's? We just used it as an excuse to hook up with guys in the back parking lot." Amanda clapped a hand over her mouth.

Michelle shrugged. "Yeah, I never spent a lot of time at Vinnie's in high school."

"I'm sorry, sweetie." Amanda pulled her close in a one-armed hug. "Teenagers can be so cruel."

Cruel enough to send hurtful emails?

Laughing, Michelle returned the hug. Amanda had been one of the girls who'd shunned her in high school, but they'd become good friends since Michelle had helped Amanda set up an accounting system for her home business a few years ago.

"Nothing much has changed. Here you are hoping to hook up with Colin Roarke, except this time it's in a restaurant, not behind it."

As they pushed through the front door of Burgers and Brews, Amanda pinched her. "Shh."

Not that anyone in the restaurant could hear Michelle's comment. The chatter from the group of people in the far corner of the room drowned out the music, and the hostess had to shout above the noise.

"Table for two?"

Michelle nodded and jerked her thumb toward the noisy crowd. "What's going on over there?"

The young hostess shrugged. "Word got out that Colin Roarke was back in town, which created a ministampede of his high school buds."

As Michelle pulled out her chair, she glanced at the clutch of people. A tall man at its center, oddly detached amid the furor, met her gaze. For whatever reason, an electric current zapped between them, and Michelle felt it down to her toes.

She averted her gaze and dropped into her chair. Must be those football-star good looks—the broad shoulders, the square jaw. She hadn't been immune to those attractions in high school, and now the man's appeal hit her like a sledgehammer all over again.

After the waitress took their drink orders, Amanda propped up her menu and peeped over the top. "They're having their own class reunion over there. Mmm-mmm, Colin looks better than ever. A few more lines on his face, but the body still looks rock hard. He's probably older, wiser…and more experienced."

"He looks…sad." Michelle shot a few glances at the group, bubbling with laughter and conversation. Colin contributed a word or a smile here and there, but he seemed aloof, separate from the people around him.

"Are you crazy? That's Colin Roarke you're talking about—football star, war hero, FBI stud."

The waitress delivered their drinks and Michelle blew on her hot tea. "Why was he a war hero? What did he do?"

Amanda wrapped her lips around the straw from her soda, staring unabashedly at Colin across the room. "I think you were in Europe on that sabbatical when all the news came through. Taliban forces captured Colin in Afghanistan. He escaped, but…"

Ducking behind her menu, Amanda hissed. "He's coming."

Colin strode past their table, a frown creasing his brow. He waved to someone behind the bar and then turned the corner to the restrooms.

"I think he noticed us." Amanda slapped the menu against the table. "Or at least you. He kept staring over here."

Michelle scoffed even though she'd felt a jolt when her eyes had met Colin's. Had he felt it, too? "Aren't you going to follow him into the bathroom?"

Amanda's eyes narrowed and she clicked her long fingernails on the side of her glass. "That's not a bad idea. I could stumble in there and pretend I thought it was the ladies' room."

The waitress took their order and apologized for the slow service. "I'm a little overwhelmed tonight."

When she walked away, Amanda shot a quick glance at herself in the mirror over the bar. "She's not the only one who's overwhelmed. I almost swooned when Colin walked past our table."

Michelle smiled into her tea. Her friend desperately wanted to feel an attraction for anyone other than her estranged husband, but Michelle could see right through her. She nodded toward the tall man striding back into the dining room. "If you were planning on following him, you're too late."

Colin crossed the room, running a hand through his short, dark hair. His gait slowed as he approached their table, and

Michelle held her breath for some absurd reason. Amanda had infected her with her silliness.

He stalled at their table, and Michelle's heart jumped. "Excuse me, ladies. Did you both graduate the same year as Tiffany Gunderson?"

Nothing personal, just business. Michelle blew out a breath and answered, since Amanda seemed uncharacteristically tongue-tied. "Yes, we did." She stuck out her hand. "I'm Michelle Girard and this is Amanda Stewart."

As he clasped her hand in a warm embrace, she noticed scars crisscrossing his wrist. Had the sadness she'd sensed led him to try something crazy?

"Of course I remember you—the girl down the block. In case you've forgotten, I'm Colin Roarke." He released her hand and Michelle had an acute feeling of loss.

He remembered her?

He turned to Amanda. "Stewart? Are you related to Sergeant Ryan Stewart of the Coral Cove P.D.?"

"Married to him." A soft pink brushed Amanda's cheeks. "Sort of."

Colin raised his brows and a crooked smile claimed his mouth. "He's a good man."

That smile set into a motion a chain of events across Michelle's body, ending in butterfly wings in her belly. Her unrequited schoolgirl crush had sneaked up on her sensible adult self.

Colin reached into the front pocket of his denim shirt and pulled out two business cards. He slid them onto the table. "I'd like to talk to you about Tiffany while I'm in town. Give me a call."

Michelle traced the edge of the card with her fingertip. "So Tiffany's death wasn't an accident? If not, why aren't the San Francisco police handling the investigation?"

A spark of interest ignited Colin's dark blue eyes. "I'd rather not discuss that here. Call me."

"Hey, Colin. Come over here and set Jeff straight on how that game with Costa ended."

Colin pinned Michelle with his dusky blue gaze and rolled his eyes. "Nice to…see you again."

Michelle chewed her bottom lip as Colin ambled back to his high school classmates, their bubbling memories sweeping him back into their circle. The favorite hometown son didn't wear the label with ease.

"We haven't been in the joint fifteen minutes and we have his card." Amanda scooped up the prize and pressed it to her breast.

"Because he wants to ask us questions about Tiffany." Michelle rubbed her thumb against the embossed letters proclaiming Colin Roarke an FBI agent. "Why do you think the FBI's involved in an investigation of Tiffany's death?"

Amanda lifted a bare shoulder. "It happened in the big city. Anything can happen there. At least we have an excuse to call him."

"How did he know we were in Tiffany's class and what would we know about her life in San Francisco?"

"Why do you have to analyze everything to death? Just sit back and enjoy, because I swear the man had his eye on you. He even remembered you from the neighborhood."

Michelle pressed her lips together as the waitress delivered their food. So Amanda had noticed that, too. Michelle hadn't had much contact with the popular Roarke boys growing up, even though the family had lived down the road. But one scene shifted into focus, and Michelle's cheeks burned with the memory.

She must've been fifteen because it happened shortly after her mother left. Michelle had retreated to her special place on the beach, a semicircle of boulders against the bluff, her own private hideaway. She hadn't cried about her mother since she'd left, but that day the tears flowed like a river of sadness.

Suddenly, her world grew darker. She'd glanced up at Colin Roarke's large form hovering at the entrance to her secret fort, blocking out the sun. He must've been home from college. He'd been surfing and his wet suit dangled around his hips. He'd asked her if she was okay, and Michelle was pretty sure she'd told him to buzz off.

Colin probably didn't remember that. Why would he?

"Told you so." Amanda tapped her fork against Michelle's water glass. "You have a very satisfied smile on your lips right now. The man is hot and he noticed you."

Michelle responded by taking a big bite of her burger.

Amanda stabbed a tomato with her fork. "I think I'd better find another friend for cruising—one who's not tall, thin and gorgeous."

"Moi?" Michelle choked down her food.

"Don't *moi* me. Ever since you got back from Paris, you look more like a fashion model than a high school math teacher."

Michelle dabbed her lips, hiding the lower half of her face behind her napkin. After Dad died a few years ago and Michelle fled Coral Cove for a summer in Paris, she *had* stepped up her game a little. She'd even gone out on a few dates, but she'd hardly describe herself as a femme fatale. She'd always shied away from that image because of Mom.

As they ate dinner and chatted around mouthfuls of food, Amanda sent fewer and fewer flirty glances toward the lively group in the corner. She pushed the last bits of lettuce around her plate and dropped her lashes. "So you think I should give Ryan another chance?"

"What's wrong? Being on the prowl isn't as exciting as you imagined? You've given up on the hometown hero already?" Michelle shoved her plate forward and planted her elbows on the table.

Amanda shook her head. "Colin's hot, but he's not my type. He's not the life of the party like I expected."

"Like Ryan."

"Yeah." Amanda managed a tremulous smile.

"Then get home and call him." Michelle waved to the waitress. As she fumbled in her wallet for money, Michelle slid a glance toward the reunion crowd, but Colin had disappeared. He must've slipped out the back, escaping from his own party.

They stepped onto the sidewalk and Michelle blinked. The fog had rolled in from the ocean, blanketing Coral Cove's main street in thick cotton. It would be even denser at her house.

"You okay to drive in this pea soup? It might be safer to walk."

"Yeah, but you live in one direction and I live in the other, so we'd have to part company here." Amanda dug her keys out of her purse. "I don't know about you, but I don't want to walk by myself in this wet blanket. Gives me the creeps."

"Just drive safely." Michelle took Amanda's arm and they stepped into the street, peering both ways.

As Michelle grabbed the car door handle, two dark figures emerged from the fog, appearing almost next to her. She gasped, pressing her body against the car.

The two teenaged boys laughed and pushed each other. "I bet the girls are hiding in the parking lot."

Michelle yanked open the door and dropped onto the seat. "Those kids scared the spit out of me."

"The girls could be hiding right in front of them, and they'd have a hard time seeing them." Amanda cranked on the engine. "Can't wait until June is over and we get some summer sunshine."

Amanda's car crawled down the street and she edged around the next turn, hunching forward in her seat. "I hope you know where your house is because I can't see a thing."

"The Vincents' house is on the right, the one with the big spotlight on their driveway. They left for a few weeks in Europe this morning." Michelle pointed to a glow, diffused by the fog. "Then there should be two streetlights on the left, and my house is at the second streetlight. Across from the streetlights, there's a long stretch of darkness where Columbella House is."

"I see the first light." Amanda eased off the accelerator. "And there's the second one."

Amanda made an abrupt illegal U-turn in the middle of the street. "Sorry to give you whiplash, but I don't want to go anywhere near Columbella House. Now *that* place gives me the creeps."

"Thanks for the ride, Amanda." Michelle grabbed the door handle and glanced back at her friend. "You left your sweater at my house. I can bring it to you later."

Amanda cut the engine. "I'd better get it now…just in case I don't go straight home tonight."

They both slid from the car, Amanda leaving her headlights on and the driver's-side door open to the street.

The headlights created a glow, spilling light on the beginning of Michelle's walkway beyond her little fence. She unlatched the gate and Amanda trailed after her.

"You really think I should call Ryan tonight?"

"Absolutely. Give him a chance to do the mea culpa. A few emails do not constitute a full-blown affair."

"I'm surprised you're so…forgiving, Michelle."

Michelle shrugged. "It's the opposite. You should be surprised if I weren't."

Amanda walked with Michelle to the front door and out of reach of the headlights. Luckily Michelle had turned on her porch light before she'd left, so she could actually put her key in the lock.

Thrusting open the door, she ducked inside and snagged Amanda's sweater from the chair. She handed it to her friend and gave her a hug. "Call him."

She watched as Amanda floated down the walkway, the fog sucking her into its embrace. Michelle waited, listening for the slam of the car door and the growl of the engine. Instead she heard…a soft thud. Fog this thick muted noise, but that didn't sound like a car door.

"Amanda?" Michelle squinted into the white wisps swirling around her. The lights from Amanda's car created a dull illumination on the sidewalk, but Michelle couldn't focus on anything beyond that. Maybe Amanda couldn't wait to get home and decided to call Ryan on her cell phone.

Michelle descended one step, her hand clutching the banister beside her. "Amanda?"

Scuffling sounds broke the eerie silence, causing the hair on the back of Michelle's neck to quiver. Her clammy hand slipped from the banister. Had Amanda tripped and fallen on the ground?

Clasping her sweater to her chest, Michelle inched down the walkway to the gate Amanda had latched behind her. Across the sidewalk, still parked in the street, Amanda's Mercedes loomed in the fog.

"Amanda, where are you?" Michelle pushed open the gate and stumbled onto the sidewalk. She walked in front of the car toward the driver's side, the door still open to the street. As she scuffed her feet along the asphalt, hands held in front of her like a blind person, her toe plowed into something soft and giving on the ground.

Michelle's heart skittered in her chest as she crouched down next to the inert form. Amanda must've fallen and injured herself. The lights from the car's interior cast a waxy glow on Amanda's pale cheek. Michelle wedged a hand beneath her friend's head and turned it toward her.

Amanda's wide, staring eyes sent a river of chills down Michelle's spine. Then she became aware of the sticky wetness oozing through her fingers.

As Michelle drew away her hand, Amanda's head lolled back revealing a dark slash across her neck.

Michelle fell backward, as a high, keening wail pierced the blanket of fog. It wasn't until she stopped to breathe that she realized the sound was coming from her own mouth.

Chapter Two

The cry, like an animal in extreme pain, shot through the fog and pierced his gut. But Colin knew human suffering when he heard it. He was intimately familiar with human suffering.

He dropped the rocks he'd been chucking into the water and lurched toward the sound. After a few seconds' break, the wail began again and he glommed onto the sound of misery like a homing device. He stumbled from the sand onto the dirt path leading to the road.

Through the veil of white mist, he discerned a car parked on the street, its headlights on and the driver's-side door open. As he jogged closer, the fog parted to reveal two figures, both on the ground next to the open door. Had there been an accident?

He heaved to a stop, his chest tight, adrenaline pumping through his system. One person lay crumpled on the ground and the other, a woman, leaned back on her arms, her head thrown back, her face twisted with anguish.

He squatted beside the nonresponsive person and jerked back. Someone had slit her throat. He'd seen her face before…at the restaurant.

He scrambled toward the other woman, Michelle Girard, and grabbed her shoulders. "What happened? Who did this?"

Her wide, glassy eyes skimmed his face as she dragged

in another breath. He shook her to dispel the shock, and the oncoming scream gurgled in her throat.

Then her gaze darted back and forth and she clutched his shirt, popping off two buttons with the strength of her grip. "He's here."

She scrambled to her feet, dragging him with her. Her body shook convulsively and her knees gave way. Before she could fall to the ground, Colin wrapped his arms around her and pulled her away from the body of her friend.

"Did you see him?"

Her head whipped around, dislodging the droplets of moisture clinging to her hair and showering his face. "No. He must still be here. I didn't hear a car. I didn't see anything."

Colin reached between their bodies and unzipped his gun bag, hanging around his waist. He withdrew his weapon and pulled Michelle toward the house with the white picket fence. "This is your house, right?"

She glanced at his Glock, and a tremble rolled through her slim frame.

"I'm Colin Roarke." He rubbed a circle on her stiff back. "Do you remember me from the restaurant a few hours ago?"

She nodded, and he propelled her toward the front door. He halted on the porch. "Did you leave your door open?"

Again she nodded, and Colin pushed over the threshold, clutching his gun. Michelle clung to his arm with her blood-stained hands as he checked the other rooms in the small house.

He grabbed her phone and called 9-1-1, and then tried to get Michelle to sit down. Shivers racked her body, and Colin knew if he released her she'd plunge to the floor.

Finally she bent her knees and perched on the edge of her couch. "It just happened. She was leaving my house. I heard noises, but I couldn't see anything. Oh, my God, he murdered her right in front of me and I didn't see a thing."

As she buried her face in her hands, Colin put his arm around her heaving shoulders. She'd been lucky the killer hadn't come after her. His muscles ached with tension. He wanted to run out there and find the SOB who had done this, but he couldn't leave Michelle.

He wouldn't leave her like he did that time when she was a kid.

Sirens blared through the night and they both jumped. Michelle jerked her head up, a shaky hand covering her mouth. "I hope Ryan's not working tonight. He can't see Amanda like that."

Colin pushed off the sofa and headed for the door. Michelle trailed after him. "You can wait inside, Michelle. Someone will come in to question you."

She twisted her hands, still smudged with traces of her friend's blood. "I can't stay inside, especially if Ryan's out there."

Colin dragged the collar of Michelle's sweater up to her pale face. "You don't need to see Amanda again. Stay in the yard."

He stepped onto the porch, tucking Michelle behind him. Three police cars and an ambulance squealed to a stop in the street. Must've emptied out the entire P.D. of Coral Cove. Did they even have a homicide detective? Colin strode forward, holding his FBI badge in front of him as the red-and-blue lights filtered through the fog.

Colin scanned the faces of the cops swarming out of their cars and didn't see Sergeant Stewart among them. But like any small-town cop off duty, he'd pick up the call on his scanner. He'd know his wife had been with Michelle Girard tonight.

The officer in charge peeled away from the surge of cops and barreled toward Colin. "What happened?"

"Mrs. Stewart dropped off Ms. Girard and somebody attacked Mrs. Stewart before she got into her car."

Michelle hovered behind Colin, hooking a finger in his belt loop. She didn't seem to be able to stand on her own without wobbling, but Colin didn't mind being her rock.

The cop smacked a hand to his forward. "Stewart? Amanda Stewart, Sarge's wife?"

"That's right, Clark. It happened in front of me, but I couldn't see a thing." Michelle had stepped forward, pulling back her shoulders, still clutching Colin's arm for support.

Another pair of headlights plowed through the fog, and tires screeched on the damp asphalt. A man's voice, frantic and hollow, echoed in the night. Sergeant Stewart stumbled into the crime scene, now illuminated with spotlights and casting an eerie yellow light on all the grim faces. He dropped onto his knees next to his wife's body and groaned.

Michelle broke away from Colin, her stride strong and purposeful. Two uniformed officers prevented her from approaching Stewart, but she called to him.

From his doubled over position, Stewart raised his head. He staggered to his feet and tripped toward Michelle. She held out her arms and Ryan crushed her body to his, burying his face in her shoulder.

His muffled voice repeated, "What happened? What happened?"

"Officer—" Colin peered at the cop's badge "—Trammell? Maybe you should question Ms. Girard inside and get Sergeant Stewart away from the crime scene."

Trammell nodded. "It's Lieutenant Trammell. You're that FBI agent, Roarke, in town to investigate Tiffany Gunderson's death, right?"

"I am."

Trammell swiped a hand across his brow. "Looks like death is following you around, Agent Roarke."

Colin clenched his teeth. *You have no idea, Lieutenant.*

Trammell yelled to one of the gawking officers. "Get County on the line now. Tell them we need a homicide detective and a CSI team." Trammell tapped Michelle on the back while he clapped his hand on Sergeant Stewart's shoulder. "Go inside, Sarge."

With her arm clasped around Stewart's waist, Michelle led him through the gate and up the brick walkway to her house.

She'd been falling apart just a few minutes ago. Now she was supporting her friend's husband with the strength of an Amazon woman. Michelle settled Stewart on the sofa and retrieved a box of tissues from the bathroom.

"Do you want some water, Ryan? Something stronger?" She shoved the tissues toward him.

"No. Nothing. What happened, Michelle?"

Stewart asked the question, but Trammell pulled out his notebook.

While Stewart alternately sobbed and cursed, Michelle recounted how Amanda had driven her home and walked to the front door to get her sweater. She grabbed one of the tissues and dabbed her nose. "She disappeared into the fog and I kept waiting for her car to start but I didn't hear it. I heard some noises and when I went out to investigate…I found her on the ground."

"Where'd you go tonight, Michelle?" Lieutenant Trammell looked up from scribbling in his notebook.

She glanced at Colin and then shifted her gaze back to Trammell. "We went to Burgers and Brews for an early dinner."

"Why there? Why tonight?" Stewart practically barked his questions, and Trammell's jaw tightened.

The tension in the air stretched as tight as a new string on a guitar. *Jealous husband?* Colin would've gone in for the kill with Stewart on edge. Trammell hadn't even asked Sergeant Stewart for an alibi, but local cops handled their own differently. The homicide detective on his way from County would take care of business.

Trammell cleared his throat. "What were you doing outside, Agent Roarke?"

"My parents have a house down the street from Ms. Girard's on the other side of Columbella. I walked there after dinner in town and was chucking rocks on the beach when I heard Ms. Girard scream."

"Did anyone else come out of their house? The Vincents? Did you see anything?"

"There was nobody on the street. I saw the parked car and the two women. I didn't want to leave Ms. Girard alone to do a search of the area. Can't see two feet in front of you in this fog, anyway."

"The Vincents are out of town." Michelle shot Colin a grateful look from beneath her dark lashes.

Taking care of Sergeant Stewart had put the soft color back into her cheeks. Being needed had given her purpose and direction. Stewart knew he could lean on her, since he'd been clutching her hand ever since they'd sat down.

Just as Michelle had leaned on him after the murder. And he'd liked someone counting on him for the first time since…

As Trammell continued his questioning of Michelle and took a sample of the blood from her hands, Colin kept his lips sealed. He had his own notions about Amanda's death, but he had more digging to do before trampling all over the local P.D.'s investigation. He'd need a closer look at the crime scene before jumping to any conclusions, and if he found the telltale sign that this murder was connected to Tiffany's and Belinda's, he could make a case to his supervisors to take over the investigation.

Because even though he'd led the CCPD to believe he was here on official business, he was actually on vacation. They didn't need to know that just yet.

Tucking his notepad back into his shirt pocket, Trammell pushed up from the sofa. "Are you going to be okay, Michelle? The team's probably going to be in front of your house for most the night, so this is the safest place to be right now."

"I'll be fine, but what about Ryan?" She squeezed the sergeant's knee and tears flooded his eyes again.

Colin tracked every detail of the sergeant's demeanor. The man had skipped right past shock into grief. How had he gotten to Michelle's house so quickly when he was off duty? He'd asked earlier why Michelle and his wife had gone to Burgers and Brews. That implied they weren't living together or Mrs. Stewart hadn't bothered to tell her husband where she was going.

Trammell studied the toes of his shiny black shoes. "Sergeant Stewart is coming to the station for some questions."

Another fat tear rolled down Stewart's cheek. Either he didn't catch the significance of Trammell's statement or he didn't care because he had nothing to hide.

A Detective Marsh from the county appeared and assured Trammell that his CSI guys were gathering evidence while the Coral Cove cops were canvassing the neighborhood.

Before taking off with Trammell to question Sergeant Stewart, Detective Marsh had a few more questions for Colin and Michelle.

Michelle told him she hadn't heard a car's engine or footsteps or any other noises after finding her friend's body. And Colin had heard only Michelle's wail. That's all he'd needed to hear to block out every other sound and sensation except for an urgent desire to trample out the source of Michelle's pain.

Colin had his own question for Detective Marsh. "Did you find anything unusual on the body? Flowers? Petals?"

"If the crime scene investigators found anything, they'd have it bagged and tagged by now, Agent Roarke. This isn't your case yet, is it?"

Colin rolled his eyes. He hated the petty politics of jurisdiction and one-upsmanship that dominated some law enforcement agencies. "Not yet, Detective Marsh."

Marsh lifted a brawny shoulder. "Then I guess you won't find out until it is yours."

Trammell and Marsh accompanied Stewart to the police department, but the coroner's van had arrived and the cops were still traversing the area. Michelle would hardly be alone, but Colin found it difficult to abandon her.

She dragged in a shaky breath and closed her eyes. "Thank you for coming when you did. H-he could've attacked again. I honestly don't think I could have moved from that spot if you hadn't come along."

"I'm glad I was outside." Colin unlatched his gun bag and settled it, heavy with his weapon, on Michelle's coffee table. "It's strange that neither one of us heard a car or footsteps running."

Her eyelids flew open and she hugged herself, her fingertips burrowing into her sweater. "Even if a Mack truck had driven by, I don't think I would've noticed."

"But I would have, and I didn't hear anything."

"By the time I found Amanda and screamed the killer had probably already run away." She hunched her shoulders. "You wouldn't have heard anything once you reached us... me."

Colin jumped from the couch and crossed the room to the

front window. He twitched back the curtain. The back doors of the coroner's van yawned open, ready for its cargo.

"Columbella House still empty?"

"Ever since... Yeah, still empty." Michelle shivered and rubbed her arms through her thick sweater.

Colin pressed his hand against the cool glass. "Maybe the killer ran for cover over there and then took off amid the noise and excitement of the police arrival."

"You mean you think he could've been at Columbella all the time we were inside waiting for the police?" Her eyes widened and she pulled her sweater tighter around her body.

Good job, Roarke, scare the lady even more.

"I don't know." Stuffing his hands in his pockets, he turned to the side and wedged his shoulder against the window. "I'm just guessing."

"Oh, God." Michelle spread her hands in front of her face. "I still have Amanda's blood on my hands."

She scrambled from the couch and ran into the kitchen. At the sink, she squeezed copious amounts of dishwashing liquid into her palm and rubbed her hands together so hard Colin expected sparks.

As the operation went on and on, Colin approached her from behind and peeked over her shoulder. Lady MacBeth-like, she continued to scour her hands under the hot water, silent tears streaming down her face and dripping off her chin.

Colin grabbed a dish towel, cranked off the water and gently clasped Michelle's shoulders, turning her toward him. He wrapped the towel around her hands, pulling her close. Then he rested his chin on top of her soft, light brown hair.

"I'm sorry about your friend. I'm sorry you found her."

She nodded beneath his chin and sniffled. "We hadn't been friends that long. We went to high school together, but we really didn't know each other until several years after we graduated. We became best friends pretty fast after that."

"And you have your ten-year reunion this summer."

"Yeah." She brought the towel to her face and used it to wipe her nose. "I don't feel much like going now."

Colin patted her back awkwardly. Her warmth and the sweet scent of her hair made him want to take her in his arms, and in her condition she just might go there willingly.

"Sit down, Michelle." He grabbed the handle of her refrigerator. "Do you want something to drink? Do you have any wine? Beer? Something to take the edge off?"

"I—I don't drink." She slid a glass from the dish drainer on the counter and filled it with tap water. Then she floated back to the couch and sank to the cushion.

"Lieutenant Trammell didn't ask you many pertinent questions. I guess because this is a small town, and he figures he knows all the answers. That homicide detective will probably call you in for more questioning." Colin dropped to the chair across from Michelle and hunched forward. "Did Amanda have any enemies? Marital problems?"

Michele took a gulp of water, and then cupped the glass between her hands. "Yeah, well, Clark Trammell already knows Amanda and Ryan are…were…separated. I'm sure he's already told Detective Marsh and they're questioning Ryan more thoroughly, but there's no way he had anything to do with Amanda's murder."

"Why were they separated?"

"Ryan sent some suggestive emails to another woman." She splayed her hands on her thighs and studied her long fingers. "The other woman lived in Colorado and I think Ryan was just flirting, but Amanda didn't see it that way."

Colin rubbed his knuckles along his jaw. "Did he ever meet this other woman, start an affair?"

"Oh, no." Michelle shook her head and her silky hair

spilled over one shoulder. "Ryan loves Amanda, but she took him for granted and I think he just needed a little validation from another woman. He had no intention of cheating."

"Sounds like you were on Ryan's side."

"I tried not to take sides, but I think a couple should try to work things out, don't you?" Michelle kept her eyes downcast, her dark lashes crescents on her cheeks.

A muscle ticked Colin's jaw as he lifted one shoulder. *Not if your fiancée cheats on you while you're overseas serving your country.*

"So maybe not the husband, but we know the killer didn't do it for money. He didn't steal her fancy car and didn't snatch her purse." Colin strolled back toward the window and parted the curtains. The coroner had left and now a tow truck had Amanda's Mercedes latched behind it.

Michelle joined him at the window, still clutching her sweater around her tall, slender frame. "I can't believe this is just some random killing. Not in Coral Cove."

"I don't believe it is random."

Turning toward him, she tilted her head. "Why are you here investigating Tiffany Gunderson's death? She died in an elevator shaft in a hotel in San Francisco. Shouldn't that be a job for the SFPD?"

Colin took a deep breath and held it. Officially, the FBI had no idea he was here in Coral Cove investigating a murder. Should he tell Michelle that Tiffany hadn't been the first Coral Cove High alumna to die a violent death? That Tiffany hadn't been the first body found with a strange yet touching calling card? Should he tell her two, now three women from her graduating class all had their lives snuffed out in an instant?

He searched her wide, dark eyes, still glassy from shock and tears. Easing out a breath, he brushed his thumb across her damp cheek, dislodging a strand of hair. "Tiffany's death involved some special circumstances. That's why I'm looking into it."

Her nostrils flared as she narrowed her eyes, no longer cloudy and unfocused. His vague explanation hadn't fooled her one bit.

She tightened her jaw and then shrugged, returning her gaze to the formless shapes scurrying back and forth in the street. "You're not at liberty to tell me anything, but I don't believe for a minute Tiffany's death was an accident. Not after tonight."

Colin ran a hand across his mouth. He'd have to watch what he said in front of Michelle because right now she didn't have to know she might be on this killer's short list of victims.

She gasped, and her hand shot out and grabbed his wrist. "Did you see that?"

No, I was watching you.

While Michelle dug her nails into his flesh, he cupped his hand around his face and peered out the glass. "I don't see anything except the cops out there wandering around."

She tapped on the windowpane and whispered. "A light at Columbella."

Chapter Three

"I don't see anything." Colin's broad shoulder pressed against hers as he leaned forward to squint into the fog-shrouded night.

Could he feel her shivering? Would he realize it had as much to do with his masculine scent and the feel of him next to her as it did with the flickering light she'd seen at Columbella House?

She clenched her teeth and released her grip on Colin's wrist. Amanda's blood hadn't even dried on the street and here she was getting giddy over a man's touch. Maybe that email had it right: *Like mother, like daughter?*

Jerking away from the window, Michelle swiped her keys from the table and scooped up a flashlight from a basket by the door. "I'm going to check it out."

"Are you crazy?" Colin grabbed her hand. "Someone just murdered your friend, and he's still out there."

"That's right. Someone just murdered my friend, practically on my doorstep, and I'm not going to sit here and do nothing." She wrestled from his grasp and jingled her house keys in her palm. "I won't be walking over to Columbella House by myself, anyway. The cops and the county CSI guy are still out there."

Now that she'd blurted out her brash statement, more from guilt than anything else, Michelle dragged her feet to the front door. She didn't really want to cross the street to Columbella House. She didn't want to go anywhere near that gloomy old Victorian, so out of place among the bungalows and beach cottages of Coral Cove.

Colin yanked his gun bag from the coffee table by its strap and hitched it around his waist. "If you saw a light at the house, I believe you. But the cops probably already canvassed that area. They might not be so anxious to cover that ground again."

Michelle released a pent-up breath. Now she could save face and actually follow through with her bold plan. She'd feel a lot safer with Colin and his gun by her side.

"Suit yourself." She shrugged and stepped onto the porch.

The spotlight still illuminated the area where Amanda had parked her car, although the car itself had been towed. The two remaining Coral Cove officers and the crime scene investigator from the county looked like they were doing more talking than investigating. A murder like this in Coral Cove would tax the resources of the small-town cops. The P.D. would have to work with the county sheriffs and if Amanda's murder had anything to do with Tiffany's murder, they'd have to call in the FBI…good thing they wouldn't have to go far to find an agent.

Shoving his hands in the pockets of his windbreaker, Colin approached the two police officers crouching next to the dark stain on the asphalt. Michelle followed him but allowed his broad back to block her view of the crime scene.

"Are you guys finished out here?" Colin swept his arm across the damp crime scene tape hanging limply in the fog.

Jerry Donnelly, one of the Coral Cove P.D. officers answered, "Yeah, we're done. Nobody else even heard Michelle's scream."

Colin faced the guy from the county. "Did you collect all the evidence?"

The guy patted the bag hanging from his shoulder. "Fingernails, hair, blood, a cigarette butt and assorted bits and pieces. Hopefully, we'll get more from the body before the autopsy is performed."

Michelle's stomach rolled and she ground her teeth together.

Colin bent down and plucked something from the ground. "You missed something."

The investigator snorted. "That's a petal. The murder occurred outside on a street. I don't know about you Fibbies, but we don't collect every twig and every speck of dirt as evidence."

"It's a rose petal. It's not a twig or a speck of dirt."

The other man pointed to the rosebushes lining Michelle's fence. "Yeah, it's a rose petal. Just like all those other rose petals on those bushes."

"It's your case…for now." Colin slipped the petal inside his pocket. "Michelle saw a light over at Columbella House. Did you guys already check over there, Officer Donnelly?"

Jerry straightened his shoulders and gave a brisk nod. "We already canvassed the yard. Nothing."

The CSI investigator shifted his bag from one shoulder to the other. "I have to go to the police department to meet with Detective Marsh. You coming?"

Jerry brushed his hands together. "We'll come with you. Michelle, are you going to be okay? You can come and stay at our place tonight."

Michelle glanced at her watch and then shifted her gaze toward Columbella. *Not much night left.* "I'll be fine. I have good, sturdy locks on my door and a phone by my bed."

"We'll send a patrol car by a few times before dawn." Jerry turned to his partner, a wide-eyed new recruit, and jerked his thumb toward the patrol car.

Michelle watched as the fog gobbled up their taillights. "I

guess they weren't interested in another look at Columbella House."

"Are you?" Colin raised his eyebrows in question.

"Sure." Michelle licked her lips. "Are you and your gun going with me?"

"Absolutely." Colin unzipped his gun bag and slid his Glock into his pocket. "Do you have that flashlight handy?"

Michelle flicked on the flashlight and waved it in front of her. They crossed the street together, and she clenched her hand at her side to keep from hooking onto Colin's arm.

He unlatched the gate and pushed it open, the rusty hinges squeaking in protest. The abandoned house peered at them through windows streaked with dirt and grime.

With his hand in his pocket, Colin crept toward the sagging porch. He pointed down and Michelle followed with the flashlight, which illuminated steps of splintered wood. "Nobody's been through this entrance for quite a while."

"I didn't see the light from inside the house. It was somewhere in the side yard."

They shuffled through the dead leaves toward the side of the house, the shaky beam of the flashlight lighting the way.

Colin tugged at the gate leading to the backyard of the sprawling house. "It's locked, Michelle. This is probably as far as the police got. And if you saw a light, it couldn't have come from the backyard. You never would've seen a light from back there."

Michelle rolled her stiff shoulders. "Maybe the light did come from the house."

"If it did, I'm not up to breaking and entering."

"Neither am I." She slumped against the gate. "Maybe I imagined the light. Maybe it was just a reflection from the police lights on the street. Columbella House has been giving me the creeps for years."

"It's a blight on the town. I wish some member of the St. Regis family would either sell the place or raze it."

"Were you still here when Kylie Grant's mother hung herself from the balcony?" Michelle shivered and pushed off the cold chain link of the gate.

"No, I wasn't. She'd copied a previous suicide. When Mia St. Regis's sister, Marissa, took off before her wedding, some said she'd killed herself, too."

"Yeah, but then both Mia and Marissa's fiancé got those letters from Marissa explaining that she and Mia's boyfriend had taken off together. I suppose the house is Mia's now. Can't blame her for not wanting to deal with it." Michelle tugged at the sleeves of her sweater. "I felt sorry for her even though she's not the type of woman who inspires pity. I guess Coral Cove Drive has seen its share of scandal."

Colin wedged a finger beneath her chin. "You had it tough in high school when your mom ran off with that senior at Coral Cove High."

Michelle blinked, afraid to meet the sympathy in his eyes. "I had it tough before that, since I was tall and skinny and wore glasses and braces."

He pinched her chin and grinned. "It didn't help that you were a bookworm and as smart as all get-out—a total bully magnet. I'm surprised you didn't escape Coral Cove like the St. Regis twins did."

"I had to take care of my dad. When Mom left with that boy, Dad collapsed."

"Do the kids still think this place is haunted?"

"Not just the kids. In fact, it makes me uneasy just standing here even if you do have a gun in your pocket." Michelle shifted away from Colin's warm touch and the toe of her shoe lodged against a stepping stone buried beneath the mulch. She tripped and sprawled onto her hands and knees, the flashlight bouncing out of her hand.

Colin dropped beside her. "Are you all right?"

"I banged my knee on a cement stepping stone. I didn't even see those before." She sat back and rubbed her throbbing knee. *You could dress up a klutz but she'd still be a klutz.*

Leaning across her body, Colin reached for the flashlight and cursed.

"What's wrong? Is it broken?"

He stepped across her and kneeled on the ground, one hand now grasping the flashlight and the other picking through the dirt and leaves. He cursed again, his body tensing.

"What did you find, Colin?" Michelle's heart banged in her chest, her breath coming out in short spurts.

He extended his hand toward her, cupping several rose petals in his palm.

Michelle swallowed. He'd seemed unusually interested in a petal he'd picked up near Amanda's body. What significance did a few rose petals have?

"They're rose petals." Her words sounded stupid hanging between them. "L-like the one at the crime scene?"

Colin jerked the beam from the flashlight across the tangled bushes bordering Columbella House. "Do you see any roses here, live ones?"

Michelle squinted into the darkness. "No, but I'm sure the Vincents have some. Dorothy Vincent is always giving me tips on mine. Couldn't the wind have blown the petals over here? What's with the petals?"

Colin hooked his arm beneath hers and pulled her up. "Let's get out of here."

Colin charged through the front yard and this time Michelle clung unabashedly to his arm until they were through the rusty front gate.

Opening his hand, Colin aimed the light at the delicate

yellow petals. "Do the Vincents have yellow roses in their yard?"

"I think so."

"And what about you? Are your roses yellow? The petal I found near the body was pink."

"I have both pink and yellow. Do you think the killer left the petals near Amanda's body? Then what? He ran across the street to Columbella House and showered more petals there?"

Michelle didn't know a thing about murder investigations, but she *was* a mathematician and she knew logic. And this didn't seem logical.

Ignoring her questions, Colin dropped to his hands and knees just outside the crime scene tape. He trailed his fingers across the ground and peeled something from the asphalt.

Holding it up to the light, he said, "It's another petal, a pink one this time. I think Amanda's murderer left the petals here and the Coral Cove P.D. didn't see them, didn't recognize them as being out of place."

Michelle folded her arms across her churning stomach. "You're scaring me, Colin. What is all this about?"

The coiled intensity of his frame relaxed and he tipped his head from side to side as if to relieve a kink in his neck. "I'm sorry, Michelle. Let's go inside."

He put his arm around her shoulders and pulled her body flush against his. His warmth seeped into her, but her teeth insisted on chattering, anyway. Colin had suspected a link between Tiffany Gunderson's death and Amanda's murder, and he'd just found it.

After Michelle unlocked her front door, Colin propelled her to the couch, pressing his hand against the small of her back. "Sit."

She sank into the corner, curling her long legs beneath her. "I'm not going to like this, am I?"

Closing his eyes, he pinched the bridge of his nose. Then he released a long breath, obviously coming to some decision. "Do you remember a girl from your class named Belinda Frank?"

The name drew a visceral response from Michelle, as a sour taste flooded her mouth and her hands curled into fists. "I remember her. You talked about my being a magnet for bullies? Well, she must have had the strongest magnetic field of all because she was the worst. She was a witch."

"Well, ding-dong, the witch is dead."

Michelle's jaw dropped as a confusing tumble of emotions swirled through her brain. "I—I didn't mean... I'd never wish..."

Colin skimmed his fingertips along her cheek. "I know that. Nobody in town knew about her death?"

"The Frank family wasn't local. They moved here Belinda's sophomore year and then moved out after she graduated. Nobody could even locate her to send an invitation to the reunion."

"One of the reasons they couldn't locate her is because she changed her name to Gigi French."

"Gigi French? Sounds like a hooker."

"She worked as a stripper in Vegas."

Michelle ran a hand through her tangled hair and closed her eyes. "How did she die?"

"Someone slit her throat and then showered her with rose petals."

Choking, Michelle hid her face in her hands. "They don't know who did it? How'd you get involved?"

"No. A buddy of mine on the Las Vegas P.D. called me because he saw the Coral Cove connection. Thought I might have known her, but she started at CCHS after I graduated. I didn't think much about it until Tiffany Gunderson fell down that elevator shaft in San Francisco. I knew the Gunderson family, so I recognized the name."

"But Tiffany's death was an accident, wasn't it?"

"I figured it was when I first heard about it, but I thought it was a weird coincidence that two young women from the same small-town high school had died violent deaths less than a month apart. So I contacted the SFPD about Tiffany's accident, and suddenly the two deaths didn't look like a coincidence."

"Why?" Michelle drew her knees to her chest and wrapped her arms around her legs to keep them from bouncing.

"Both women graduated the same year...and there were rose petals in the elevator shaft."

Michelle leaned her forehead on her knees, not even minding the pain from her bruises. "So the FBI sent you back home to investigate?"

Colin cleared his throat. "Not exactly."

Turning her head to the side, Michelle asked, "What does that mean?"

"Technically, I'm on vacation. The FBI didn't send me here."

"Great. So this is all off the record and below the radar?"

"That's right."

"But now that the killer has struck again, this could be a case for the FBI. A serial killer in different states? Sounds like a job for the Feds to me."

Colin stretched his arms above his head and yawned, and Michelle's gaze dropped to the muscles shifting across his chest and bunching his shoulders. He looked even better than he had as a cocky teenager.

"It might be a job for the Feds, but not necessarily for this Fed. The FBI doesn't usually assign agents to cases in their hometowns."

"What are you going to do?" Michelle sucked in a breath

and held it. She didn't want another agent on the case. She wanted Colin Roarke to stay right here in Coral Cove. In fact, she wanted him camping outside her house.

The corner of his mouth lifted. "I'm staying on vacation in Coral Cove, but I can use a little help since I won't be with my regular partner. Do you have any idea why someone might be killing the female graduates of your class?"

"Me?" Michelle's voice squeaked in a totally embarrassing manner. "You want my help?"

He tapped the side of his head. "You were the smartest girl in your class. Can you think of any reason why these three were targeted?"

"I have no idea. Tiffany and Amanda hung out with the same crowd and were both cheerleaders, but Belinda wasn't really part of that group." She slid her legs from beneath her and propped her feet on the coffee table. "Besides, you're asking the wrong CCHS Dolphin. I didn't hang with that crowd, either, and I don't know what they might have been into. I didn't become Amanda's friend until later."

"But you know who *was* in that clique. Can you give me a list of names?"

"Sure." Michelle's heart skipped a few beats at the thought of helping Colin with this case. She wanted Amanda's killer brought to justice, and she had every confidence Colin was the man to do it.

Colin pointed to the weak light pressing against the front windows. "We've been up all night. I don't know about you, but I usually need some sleep before I can function. Will you be okay here alone?"

"I'll be fine." Michelle scrambled from the couch. "Like you said, it's morning, and once the news of Amanda's murder gets out, Coral Cove Drive is going to resemble Grand Central Station. I probably won't be alone here for days."

"That's a good thing." Colin snapped his gun bag around his waist and shuffled toward the door. Grabbing the handle he turned and she almost ran into his chest. "Be careful, Michelle. You may not have run with that bunch, but you graduated with them."

Michelle twisted her fingers in front of her. "I'll be careful, and you need to find Amanda's killer. She didn't deserve that." She waved a hand toward the street, tears pooling in her eyes, her nose stinging.

Colin hugged her, drawing her head onto his comfortable shoulder. Closing her eyes, Michelle wound her arms around his waist. He smelled tangy and fresh like the sea.

She mumbled into his chest. "Thanks for everything, Colin. I don't think I could've gotten through this night without you."

He drew back and wiped a tear from her face with the rough pad of his thumb. "I don't know. I think I might have added to your grief and pain."

"No. If I'm going to help Amanda, I need to know everything. And if I'm a target for this maniac, I need to know that, too."

"You've turned into quite a woman, Michelle Girard." He touched his finger to her nose, dropped it to her lips and then stepped into the overcast morning.

A few hours of fitful sleep later, Michelle stumbled into her bathroom to shower and then changed into a pair of shorts and a T-shirt. The events of last night seemed like a dream, and she crept to her front window to make sure it had all really happened.

She staggered and clutched the windowsill as the reality of Amanda's murder hit her like a wrecking ball to the gut. A crowd of people ringed the police tape, staring at the bloodstain on the street. Amanda's blood.

She wanted to scream at them, shoo away the vultures.

While she'd been sleeping, she'd heard her doorbell ring and a few knocks on the door. They'd question her endlessly about last night.

Michelle rubbed her eyes and retreated to her kitchen, where she cooked some eggs and made toast. Once she'd eaten, she wrapped her hands around a cup of steaming tea and tiptoed to her front door again and peeked out the window.

People still mingled in the street, forming clutches of gossip groups and then breaking apart to form new groups. Michelle took a few steadying breaths before opening her front door. She'd have to face them sooner or later.

She stepped onto her front porch, taking a sip of fragrant, hot tea. The overcast morning looked a little brighter than it had the past few weeks, giving hope that the sun might struggle through today. Would Colin have another look at Columbella House by the light of day? She wanted to be there with him.

She squinted as a news van parked on the street. The newshounds sure hadn't wasted any time. A man scrambled from the passenger side of the van and waved his hands over his head.

"Ms. Girard! Can we talk to you?"

"No!" She stepped forward, cupping her hand around her mouth and yelled again. "No!"

As her bare feet moved to the edge of her porch, her toes met some damp leaves. She glanced down. She gasped and dropped her cup.

The brown tea sailed through the air, splashing her feet… and scattering rose petals.

Chapter Four

Michelle stifled a scream. She didn't want the reporter to notice anything. Her heavy ceramic cup, its handle chipped, rocked back and forth on the porch. She crouched down, her toes inches from the petals clinging to the damp wood.

She snatched up her scarred cup and swung around, ready to grab a broom and sweep the petals from her porch. She halted midturn and closed her eyes. Evidence. Those petals represented more evidence for Colin. Not that he wouldn't believe her, but she wanted him to see them with his own eyes.

She wanted to see him with her own eyes.

"Good morning, Michelle. Are you okay?"

Michelle looked up at the sidewalk. Tyler, Mayor Tyler Davis, plowed through the little gate, ignoring the reporters, and strode up the path, his arms swinging purposefully by his sides.

Michelle shuffled closer to the petals as if to protect them from Tyler's wingtips. He still hadn't figured out that he was the mayor of a small beachside town, not a big city.

"Hello, Tyler." She curled her fingers around the chipped mug handle, the rough edge biting into her hand. "I still can't believe it happened."

"Amanda should've never left Sergeant Stewart." He shook his head.

Michelle's nostrils flared and her fingers tightened on the cup's handle. "You're not blaming Amanda for getting murdered, are you?"

"Of course not. But if she'd…" He eyed Michelle's face, so tight she felt as if one quick grimace would shatter it. Tyler waved his hands. "It's a terrible business, and you were so close you could've witnessed the whole thing if the fog hadn't been so thick last night."

A tingle traced a line up her spine and she hunched her shoulders. "I couldn't see a thing. I just can't believe it."

"Not great timing for the summer rush, either."

"You did *not* just say that."

"Say what?"

Michelle jerked her head up and relief spread through her body like a drug. The news van was pulling away and Colin latched the gate behind him, crowding Tyler on the first step.

Tyler shuffled a few steps to the side.

Michelle leveled a finger at Tyler. "Mayor Davis here thinks Amanda's murder is bad timing for the summer tourist season."

Colin raised his brows and stared down at Tyler's reddening face.

"I didn't mean it like that, Michelle." He thrust out his hand toward Colin. "Good to see you back in town, Roarke. Do you remember me?"

Colin clasped Tyler's hand. "Sure, I remember the Davis family. You own a bunch of property downtown."

"That's right. Still do." Tyler brushed a speck of dust from his sleeve. "I'm the mayor of Coral Cove now."

"Are you here in an official capacity, Mayor?"

"Official?" Tyler rubbed his chin as if thinking it over. "Everything in Coral Cove is my business, but I'm here as a friend to Michelle."

Michelle pursed her lips. She'd always figured Tyler had

constituents, not friends. And right now the only friend she needed was Colin. She shifted her eyes to the damp rose petals still clinging to the porch. Then she blew out a breath.

"Thanks, Tyler, but Colin is here on official business, so…" She waved a hand vaguely in front of her as if to shoo the mayor off her porch.

Tyler captured her fingers and squeezed them in a clammy grasp. "Let us know if you need anything, Michelle."

"I will." She slipped her hand out of his clutches and slid the tips of her fingers in the back pocket of her shorts.

Tyler shook hands with Colin again and sauntered down the walkway, his spine stiff with self-importance.

Colin snorted. "Could the guy get any more officious?"

"Don't ask."

"I'm not really here on official business you know." Colin slouched against the wooden post supporting the awning above the porch.

"Yes, you are."

He jerked to attention. "You know something I don't know?"

"Look down." Michelle pointed to the petals on the porch in case Colin had forgotten his directions.

His gaze followed her pointing finger, and a quick intake of breath told Michelle he'd picked up on the significance. He crouched, his knee balancing on the first step.

"When did you notice these?"

"This morning when I came out to survey the hordes." She tilted her chin toward the groups of people on the street, gawking around the yellow crime scene tape.

He stirred the petals with his fingertip. "They're the same color as your roses. Someone could've tracked them up to your porch, carrying them on the soles of their shoes."

Bending over to study the petals, she inhaled Colin's fresh, masculine scent. It smelled better than the sweet roses, and her cheeks warmed when he met her gaze with his piercing blue eyes. Their intensity made her fear that he could see straight into her soul and read her thoughts.

"Well, that's a logical explanation." She tapped her fingernails on the chipped mug. "And here I thought a killer had left his calling card."

Colin cupped her elbow as he rose, bringing her with him. Still maintaining eye contact, he said, "I don't think we can rule out your first assumption."

A tremble rolled through her body. Colin must've felt it because he squeezed her elbow and ran his palm up her inner arm. His touch caused her nerve endings to riot and she shivered again.

"D-do you think it's a warning?" She pulled away from him and hugged herself. Not that Colin's arms wouldn't have felt a whole lot better, but he hadn't come here to comfort her. Had he?

"I think you need to be careful." He brushed his hands together and shoved them in the pockets of his jeans.

"I told Tyler you were here on official business just to get rid of him." She inspected the handle of her cup so he wouldn't see the hope in her eyes. She hadn't been a silly twit in high school and she didn't plan to take on that role now. "Why did you drop by?"

His hands burrowed deeper in his pockets as he hunched his shoulders. "I wanted to check up on you. Rough night."

"Thanks." Pleasure fizzed through her veins, pooling in all the right places. She could get used to a man like Colin Roarke looking out for her.

Michelle jerked her thumb over her shoulder. "Do you want to come inside and have some coffee? Tea?"

"Sure." He pointed at the brown puddles on the porch. "Looks like you could use more tea yourself."

"When I saw the petals on my doorstep, I dropped my

cup. It didn't occur to me at first that someone could've brought them up here on the bottom of his shoe." She shoved open the screen door, and Colin followed her into the house, dwarfing the small room with his large frame.

"You have reason to be jumpy."

"Tea okay or are you a coffee drinker?" She held up the copper teapot.

"Tea's fine." He hunched over the counter, making his shoulders look broader than ever.

Looked broad enough to accommodate all her worries, but he hadn't come here to give her an excuse to fall apart. He'd probably had a lifetime of people dependent on his strength.

"You know, I had enough people traipsing up to my door this morning. There are probably rose petals strewn up and down the entire length of my walkway."

"I'm checking out the house today."

"What?" She clanged the teapot onto the stove top with unexpected force.

"Columbella House. I'm checking it out. It was too dark to see anything last night, but it would've made a great hiding place for someone looking to get away in a hurry."

Folding her arms, Michelle wedged her hip against the counter. "I'm coming with you."

"You sure?"

"I'd rather know what's over there than not." She dug her fingers into her upper arms. "Amanda was my friend. I can't sit around and do nothing. Maybe if I'd walked her out to her car…"

"Then you might both be dead." He came around the counter, joining her in the kitchen, crowding her. "Don't blame yourself, Michelle. It's a useless exercise."

Blue-gray clouds scudded across his eyes, veiling them. Again, she sensed a deep sadness lurking behind the confidence and courage. The caretaker in her wanted to banish his sadness.

As if she had that power.

She turned toward the cupboard and grabbed two cups from the shelf. "I guess…it's like stories of survivors. There's always that sense of guilt, isn't there? I wonder if it ever completely goes away."

Colin was so close behind her the warmth of his body penetrated her cotton T-shirt. When he spoke, his breath stirred the tendrils of her hair.

"I don't know if it does."

She reached for her tin of tea bags. "Earl Grey okay?"

"Earl Grey?"

She turned and Colin took a step back, blinking, as if coming out of a trance. She held up the foil pouch. "Earl Grey? You're not much of a tea drinker, are you?"

"Coffee man."

"You could've told me." She ripped into the pouch and dropped the tea bag into a cup. "I can make coffee."

He lifted one of those square football-player shoulders. "I'm a low-maintenance guy. Besides, I came over here to make sure you got through the night okay, not to demand breakfast."

The kettle whistled and Michelle poured the boiling water over the tea bags. "I'm glad you stopped by, and brewing a pot of coffee would have been a small price to pay for the chance to search the house…with you."

He thanked her for the mug of tea, and then blew on the surface of the liquid.

She averted her gaze from his puckered lips. Slurping her own tea, she burned her tongue. "Are we going to wait until the vultures out there scatter before sneaking into Columbella House?"

He crossed the room and flicked the curtains at the window. "Are they ever going to scatter?"

She joined him, her shoulder brushing his. "Believe it or not, the crowd's a lot smaller than it was earlier."

"We'll go around the side of the house. Nobody has to know we're there."

"So we *are* sneaking."

He cocked his head at her, one side of his mouth curving into a smile. "Does that make it more appealing to you?"

"This is a small town. People talk."

"I think we're both aware of that."

She took a sip of her tea, hiding the bottom half of her face with the mug. "People said good things about you."

"People say good things about you, too, Michelle. It was just your mother, and you're not your mother."

Not according to those emails. "I know, but when your parent screws up, the trash gets heaped on you, as well."

"What your mom did is in the past, and I've heard nothing but people singing your praises since I've been back."

"You must be talking to the parents of my students. They like that I hold their kids' feet to the fire in algebra."

He blew out a noisy breath and ruffled the back of her hair. "You make it hard on a guy to pay you a compliment."

She ducked her head, embarrassment warming her cheeks. That's what Amanda always used to tell her. Pain sliced through her left temple and she pressed the mug to her head.

"Are you okay?"

"Let's get over to Columbella House and see if we can find something. Amanda didn't deserve to die in the street like that."

Michelle put their cups in the sink and dragged a hoodie from a hanger in the closet. "I'm sure it's cold in that old house. I don't think anyone's been in there since the twins were last here."

"And they haven't been back?"

"Mia's in New York and nobody's heard from Marissa since she took off with Mia's boyfriend."

Colin grinned. "I remember Mia's temper. If I were Marissa I wouldn't come back, either."

Michelle crouched by the front door and plucked the flashlight she'd used last night from the basket. "I don't think the electricity is on over there."

Colin opened the door for her. When he stepped onto the porch, he shoved the rose petals off the step with the toe of his shoe.

Michelle unlatched the front gate and pushed through, keeping to the sidewalk and avoiding the people on the street.

"Michelle!"

Darn. Not fast enough.

She cranked her head around and spotted Ned Tucker, the high school football coach, peeling away from the group.

"Did you see anything last night?"

She shook her head, shoved her hands in her pockets and continued up the sidewalk with Colin close behind her.

He took her arm. "Let's cross here like we're heading toward the beach path."

On one side of Columbella House, a path led down to a rocky beach. A cave was carved out in the rocks and teenagers hung out there even as they avoided the ramshackle house.

A gate hanging from one hinge separated the sidewalk from the path, and Colin unlatched it and shuffled onto the sandy path.

Instead of taking the winding trail down to the beach, he

hopped over the dilapidated fence that enclosed the side yard of Columbella House.

Although the fence was low, Colin lifted Michelle to the ground on the other side. They stood silently in the yard, listening to nothing but the sound of the waves crashing below them.

And the thud of Colin's heart beneath her cheek.

A strange sense of lethargy seeped into Michelle's bones. She didn't want to move from this spot, encircled in Colin's arms, protected, safe. Once they moved, the magic spell would dissipate like sea spray.

Colin cleared his throat and gave Michelle's waist a squeeze. Not that he couldn't stand here forever holding Michelle close and inhaling the scent of wildflowers that clung to her hair. "Let's try to get in through the side door."

She jumped back, as if his words had startled her, had dragged her out of some dreamworld. He'd gladly return there with her, but right now he had a murder to investigate. And he had to do it before his vacation ended.

He kept hold of her hand and led her through a tangle of weeds and tall grass. He motioned toward a side door sporting a broken window. "Looks like someone already had the same idea."

He jiggled the door handle, but it was locked. "Can I borrow your sweatshirt? I promise to replace it if it rips."

Michelle raised her brows and dangled the sweatshirt from her fingertips.

Colin tucked his hand and arm into the hood of the sweatshirt and plunged into the hole in the glass. He grappled for the dead bolt and turned it, and then felt for the door handle. He turned it once, popping the lock.

He shook out Michelle's sweatshirt. "Thanks. Not one tear."

"I knew there was a good reason to bring it."

Colin opened the side door and poked his head inside the house. "It's the kitchen."

He stepped onto the chipped tile. Someone had already shoved aside the pieces of glass from the broken window. Considerate.

Michelle wrinkled her nose. "It smells musty."

"Thanks to the ocean, it smells a lot better than I expected. At least that broken window let in some fresh air." He poked around the kitchen, but the previous residents had left nothing there. "Did the twins actually live here the last time they were in town?"

Michelle opened the fridge, pinched her nose and slammed the door shut. "No. I think Mia was going to try to fix things up a bit, but after her boyfriend took off with her sister, she abandoned that idea along with the house and went back to New York."

"Is there anything in the fridge?"

"Just that unused fridge smell." She peered into the hallway. "No sense in searching this big house together. It'll take half the time if we split up. Just tell me what to look for."

"You sure you're okay looking around here by yourself?"

Michelle straightened her shoulders. "I'm good. If there's anyone else in here, I'll make a run for it…and you have a gun."

"You take the upstairs and have a look in the bedrooms and bathrooms up there. I'll stay on this floor and head down to the basement. Just be on the lookout for anything new. I mean any sign that someone has been here recently."

"Rose petals?"

He nodded and squeezed her hand before she headed for the staircase.

"And be careful on those stairs." He rubbed a hand across his mouth, feeling like an idiot. Michelle was a grown woman, not a shy teen anymore.

He turned his attention to the search. Columbella House had been beautifully crafted and designed. It was a shame it had been left to ruin, but the house had a reputation.

Bad things happened here.

He snorted. He was as pathetic as the superstitious residents of Coral Cove, avoiding the house and calling for its demolition. The mayor was probably on that bandwagon.

He ran a hand along the intricately carved banister, his fingers clearing a trail in the dust. He called upstairs. "You okay up there?"

Michelle's muffled reply floated down. "I'm okay. You?"

"Going to look around a little more and then head for the basement."

She didn't respond, so he finished wandering through the dining room, the living room, another sitting room, a library and a half bathroom. Nothing amiss.

He pushed open the basement door and flicked on the flashlight Michelle had given him. A flight of stairs tumbled into the darkness below. He aimed his beam of light on the first step and grasped the scarred wooden handrail. He tested the step with his weight and continued downstairs, the chilly air wrapping its fingers around him the farther he descended.

That fresh ocean breeze hadn't permeated the depths down here. The dank smell of mold and water rot assaulted his nostrils.

When he reached the bottom step, he aimed his flashlight into the four corners of the room. The sword of light cut across generations of beach paraphernalia—tattered umbrellas, broken beach chairs, deflated inner tubes and air mattresses. Their bright colors muted and depressed by the darkness shrouding their final resting place.

Colin shuffled across the floor, his footsteps the first to imprint the dust in many years. He poked through the long-forgotten summer accoutrements. Nobody had been hiding down here.

He brushed his hands on the thighs of his jeans and turned back toward the stairs. As the beam of light tripped up the steps, something glimmered on the floor.

Colin crouched in front of the staircase and reached between the steps. He ran his fingers across the cement. They stumbled over a chain of some sort. As he scooped it up, the hair on the back of his neck quivered.

MICHELLE SMILED AS SHE PUSHED through the door of the first bedroom after the bend in the hallway. Colin's concern for her well-being sent tingles along her skin. And the fact that he'd taken the basement sent a wave of relief through her body. No way did she want to head down those stairs into the darkness.

The bedrooms at Columbella surprised her with their order. A thick layer of dust coated everything in sight, but the grime couldn't hide the beautiful lines of the furniture, and all the beds sported full linen, including matching bedspreads, shams and pillows.

She lifted a flounced duvet and peered under the bed. She strode to the closet and sneezed as she flung open the doors. Empty hangers swayed on a rod, boxes sat in neat rows on the floor.

She exited the room and a creaking noise from the next bedroom slowed her gait. Probably just the floorboards protesting her intrusion.

Despite her commonsense approach, her heart skittered in her chest as she eased open the door. She glanced over her shoulder, longing for Colin's reassuring voice.

She shuffled into the room. Her gaze darted toward the bedspread, wrinkled and wavy with indentations. She ducked and peered under the bed. Dust bunnies scurried into the corner.

She slid a sidelong glance at the closet, almost wishing she could ignore the sliver between the two doors. Every other closet door in every other bedroom had been closed. Holding her breath, she tiptoed to the closet.

"Colin?" She licked her dry lips. He was probably in the bowels of the house…the spooky part. She squared her shoulders and whipped open the closet door.

Her mouth dropped open and she stumbled backward. She hit the bedpost. The jolt of the collision cut through her shock and she let loose with a scream that had to be piercing straight through the floors to the basement.

Chapter Five

The shaggy man in the closet spread his arms wide and smiled. "Caught me."

Michelle crossed her arms over her chest as if to ward off a blow or a bullet...or the man's pungent odor. His hands were empty, but that didn't mean anything. He could have a hidden weapon or he could strangle her with his bare hands.

She choked and spun around, colliding with Colin as he charged through the door, his weapon grasped in one hand.

He gripped her arm with the other hand to steady her. "What happened? What's wrong?"

She thrust a shaky finger at the closet where the disheveled stranger still hadn't moved. "He's in there."

Colin shoved her toward the door and strode toward the closet. He flung the doors wide and leveled his gun at the man slouching amid the dresses and skirts.

"Get out now and put your hands where I can see them. Call 9-1-1, Michelle."

She patted the pockets of her shorts and dragged out her cell phone. While she breathlessly relayed the pertinent information to the dispatcher, the man in the closet inched a tentative foot forward.

"Be careful, Colin." The fact that Colin had the man at gunpoint didn't ease her fears.

Colin gestured with his gun. "Hurry up and keep your hands in front of you."

The man shuffled forward a few more steps, his arms held out. He started whistling.

Michelle sucked in a breath. Was it some sort of signal? She dipped into the hallway and looked both ways.

The man stood before Colin and peered at him through a veil of stringy hair. His filthy clothes hung on his gaunt frame, his lips, still puckered in song, framed by a wild beard. He dropped his arms to his sides and his hands nestled amid the folds of his raggedy clothing.

Colin steadied the metal-gray barrel of the gun. "Put your hands back in front of you where I can see them."

The man gave him a gap-toothed smile. "I had a gun once. Don't have it no more."

"Let me see your hands. Real slow."

The man hunched his narrow shoulders and raised his arms again. He held his hands, tipped with dirty fingernails, in front of him where they trembled. "Is that what you want, boss?"

"What are you doing here?"

"Is this your house, boss?"

Colin's jaw tightened. "No."

"Not mine, either."

"So what are you doing here?"

Michelle glanced at the time on her cell phone. The police had a mile to get here at high speed. Where were they?

The man moved his hand toward his face, and Colin's finger tightened on the trigger.

He scratched his beard and turned his head toward Michelle. "I scared the pretty lady, huh?"

Michelle nodded, and her heartbeat began to return to normal. He seemed harmless enough now, but maybe Colin's big gun had something to do with that impression.

Sirens wailed in the distance, and the grungy man swore. "You didn't have to go and call the cops on me. I didn't do nothing wrong. Just scared her. Wasn't even trying. Heard her going through the rooms and figured I'd better wait it out in the closet. Didn't know she'd go snooping in the closet."

Colin narrowed his eyes. The hand on his gun seemed to relax, or at least his knuckles were no long the color of white marble.

Michelle shifted her gaze to Colin's face. Was he thinking what she was thinking? This man with his long hair, over-grown beard and disheveled clothing didn't fit the profile of Amanda's killer. And he definitely wasn't responsible for the murders in Vegas and San Francisco.

Colin repeated his previous question. "What are you doing in this house?"

Waving his arms at his sides, the man said, "It's empty, isn't it? I needed a place to crash."

Several pairs of footsteps charged up the stairs. "Michelle? Roarke? You up here?"

Colin backed up to the door, keeping in front of her and keeping his gun trained on the homeless man. "In here."

His own gun drawn, Chief Evans barreled through the door almost knocking Michelle's shoulder. "Face down. Prone position."

Colin lowered his weapon and shook his head. "I think he's just a homeless guy camping out."

Another officer had joined the chief and shoved the stranger onto the hardwood floor. The cop dragged the man's arms behind his body and snapped a pair of cuffs on him.

The homeless man started whistling again.

"We'll take it from here, Roarke. Looks like we just might have our man."

Colin cleared his throat. "I think…"

The chief hustled the stranger past Michelle and Colin. "We'll handle it."

The man winked at Michelle as Chief Evans shoved him out the bedroom door. Another officer squeezed past Colin into the bedroom.

"Did he have a weapon? Did he hide anything in here?"

"We didn't get that far. I think the dude's just a homeless guy looking for some temporary shelter."

"Chief thinks we just nailed Amanda's killer." The officer pulled a pair of gloves out of his pocket. "I'm going to do a thorough search of the room. Thanks for your assistance. You can leave now. The chief knows you're not officially on the Gunderson case, Roarke."

Colin glanced at Michelle and rolled his eyes. "Come on."

He steered her through the front door, which was now standing open. The curious folks from down the street gawking over Amanda's murder site had shifted their attentions to Columbella House and the scruffy man now being stuffed into the backseat of a Coral Cove P.D. squad car.

Michelle gulped in a few breaths of salty air. "He's not Amanda's killer, is he?"

Colin wandered to the side gate, grabbed the top and leaned forward, peering at the path that rambled to the beach. "No."

"Maybe—" Michelle twisted the arms of the sweatshirt that she'd wrapped around her waist "—he's mentally ill. He could've been on his way to Columbella, stumbled across Amanda getting in her car and just gone off."

He turned his head and raised one brow. "Did that guy look capable of attacking someone the way Amanda was attacked?"

"You mean sneaking up on her and slitting her throat." Michelle kicked at the weeds clinging to the gate, sending puffs of dandelion floating through the air.

He brushed the back of his hand along her fingers where she'd hooked them, like claws, onto the chain-link fence. "I'm sorry."

She sniffled and blinked. "No. He didn't look capable of kicking a cat. He'd fall over. But that's not going to stop Chief Evans or Mayor Davis from railroading this guy. He'll be languishing in some jail cell just in time for the summer tourists to start flooding Coral Cove."

"That's stupid." His fingers curled around hers. "If they're that shortsighted, they just might allow the real killer to walk. And maybe strike again."

Michelle shivered. "You think I'm on his list?"

"I know you graduated the same year as the other women."

"The three murders could be completely unrelated—a coincidence."

"And the petals?"

"The petals." The terror from this morning when she'd seen the rose petals on her porch punched her in the gut. She sagged.

"Let's get out of here." Colin peeled her fingers from the gate and laced his own with hers.

They skirted the lingering knots of people in the street and Michelle tugged on his hand. "So which is it, Colin? Do you believe the killer scattered those petals on my porch or do you believe some innocent bystander carried them there on the bottom of his shoes?"

Colin wanted to reassure her, drive the fear from her big, brown eyes, but he couldn't lie to this woman. He couldn't pretend that she didn't face some danger from this wily killer.

"If it's the former, I'll make sure he never gets that close to you again." He tightened his grip on her hand.

A bicycle wobbled down the street between pedestrians,

and the bespectacled rider raised his hand in salute. Michelle waved back, and Colin blew out a breath. What now? Couldn't he ever get this woman alone? He had some more reassuring to do.

The cyclist pulled up beside them and shoved the glasses up his nose. "Michelle, are you okay? I heard what happened this morning and that it happened right outside your front door."

The man lurched off the seat of his bike, straddling it with his feet planted firmly on either side. His gaze dipped to their clasped hands, and Michelle disentangled her fingers from Colin's.

"It was horrible, Alec. I can't believe it happened. I can't believe Amanda's gone."

Alec extended his hand to Colin. "I'm Alec Wright."

"I'm sorry." Michelle tilted her head toward Colin. "This is Colin Roarke. Colin, this is Alec Wright. We teach at the high school together."

For a skinny guy Alec had a strong grip. Then Colin noticed Alec's legs encased in Lycra bicycle shorts and realized the guy was wiry, not skinny. But he still wore Lycra bicycle shorts. "Good to meet you."

"I've seen your name all over the school. Yours and your brother's. Kieran, right?"

"Right." At the mention of his brother's name, Colin's face tightened. Would it always be this way? Would he ever be able to think about his brother without this pain shooting into his gut?

Alec's eyes widened behind his wire-rimmed glasses. "I—I've seen your names on a lot of trophies in the trophy case."

Colin shrugged. "Don't know why they don't replace those old things with new trophies."

"Because they're school records." Alec cocked his head at Colin as if studying some strange specimen.

"Whatever." The guy annoyed him. He needed to take his Lycra and ride away.

Michelle drew her eyebrows over her nose. "If you have some time this weekend, Alec, maybe you can look at my laptop for me. I have a couple of questions about my email."

"Yeah, sure." Alec blushed as red as his bike. "Give me a call. I'd be happy to help."

Of course he would. The guy had a crush on Michelle as far as he could stretch his stretchy pants.

"Nice meeting you." Colin jerked his thumb toward Michelle's house. "We gotta…"

"Oh, sure. Oh, yeah. I'm glad you're okay, Michelle. Sorry about Amanda." He clambered onto his bike and headed toward the coast highway.

Colin squinted after him. "Didn't sound sorry about Amanda."

"He and Amanda never got along." She dug her hands into her hips. "What is wrong with you? Did you take an instant dislike to Alec or something? He's a nice guy and a good teacher."

"I didn't like his bicycle shorts."

Her chocolate-drop eyes studied his face. "You didn't like that he mentioned your trophies—yours and Kieran's."

He didn't like that he'd mentioned Kieran, period.

He shrugged. "Don't know why they keep those things around."

They'd been walking and talking and had wound up at Michelle's front door. She unlocked the door and shoved it open. Colin didn't even wait for an invitation as Michelle stepped across the threshold, still talking.

"You should be proud of those trophies. Heck, if the school gave trophies for academic excellence, I wouldn't mind a few of those scattered around with my name on them."

Colin laughed, rubbing the last of the kinks out of his neck. "You were a brain, weren't you?"

She stuck out her tongue. "Go ahead. You can say it. I was a nerd, complete with glasses and braces and bony chest."

As if pulled by a magnetic force, his gaze dropped to the gentle curve of her breasts beneath her cotton T-shirt. By the time he'd trained his eyes back to her face, a rosy blush had claimed her cheeks.

"The years have been kind."

She giggled and spun around. The compliment had made her uncomfortable. A truth smacked against his forehead and made its way to his lips. "You played up the nerd persona in high school, didn't you? Because of your mom."

She froze and her back stiffened. "That's ridiculous. Why would you think any high school girl would want to be a geek?"

"Any high school girl who had a hootchie-cootchie mama."

Her eyes flashed fire as she turned on him. "You're... you're..."

"Despicable." He'd been so excited to discover something about Michelle, so intrigued to have chipped through her cool exterior, he'd lost all sense of social etiquette. "I'm sorry, Michelle. I had no right."

She blew out a breath and dragged a hand through her thick hair. "No. You're right. I wanted to put as much distance as possible between me and my mom. I didn't want people thinking I was anything like her."

Her dark eyes pooled. He preferred the fire. In two strides, he was at her side. He slid a knuckle beneath her chin and a tear dangled on the end of her long lashes. "I'm an idiot."

Her lush lips trembled into a smile. "You're an astute idiot. The only person I'd ever admitted that to was Amanda."

The tear dripped onto her cheek, and he halted its downward path with his thumb. "I'm going to find this guy, Michelle. And he's not some whistling homeless dude."

Sniffling, she pulled back her shoulders. "I—I might have another clue."

"Something you remembered?" He stepped back from her warmth, squashing his desire, shelving it…for later.

"Emails."

"Emails?"

She ducked around him and headed for her kitchen table. "It actually occurred to me before, but I was too embarrassed to tell you about it. But now that my pathetic insecurities are out in the open, I may as well lay it all out there."

She didn't have the corner on pathetic insecurities.

"Has someone been threatening you?" That's why she was calling in the help of the bicycle geek. The fact that she'd planned to open up to Alec before him irritated the hell out of him.

"Sort of… I don't know." She hovered over her laptop, clicking keys on the keyboard. "Darn. I should've been saving them."

He joined her at the table as she scrolled through her inbox. "What did the emails say?"

"I was too chicken to open them." She drummed her fingers on the tabletop. "But the subject line said, *Like mother, like daughter?*"

"That sounds like a threat to me. Or at least harassment." He sat in front of the computer and opened her Deleted Items.

"Don't bother. I did a hard delete and sent them to cyberspace oblivion."

"Do you think Bicycle Boy can help?"

She huffed and punched him in the arm. "He's a good guy."

"I hope he knows how to retrieve those messages." He rubbed his biceps where her delicate hand had nailed him. "Do you know if Amanda had been receiving any emails? Any threats?"

"She didn't mention anything to me." She hugged herself and wedged a hip against the kitchen table. "Amanda didn't have any enemies."

"Had she been on any dates since the separation from her husband?"

"No. She talked a good game, but she missed Ryan." Michelle's face tightened and she pursed her lips. If she was going to burst into tears, he had a strong shoulder.

Her cell phone played some hip-hop song and Colin raised his brows.

"I like to keep current with the kids." She answered the phone and moved to the window.

Colin clicked around Michelle's computer as she talked in a low voice across the room. He'd have to give over to Alec's computer skills and hope the guy knew what he was doing and could retrieve those messages. Maybe someone was trying to scare Michelle, put her on edge. Killers played games, especially the smart ones.

"That was Chief Evans. He wants to see me this afternoon. You, too."

"Is he still convinced he has his man?"

"He wouldn't go into it with me."

"Any luck?" She pointed at the laptop screen.

"No. I'm going to have to defer to Alec. Dammit."

She shook her head. "I don't know why you took an instant dislike to Alec. He's harmless."

Harmless is not the way Colin would describe the way Alec had looked at Michelle. Did the woman have no clue how sexy she was? She'd probably be uneasy to hear herself described as sexy...thanks to that mother of hers. *Hootchie-cootchie mama.* What had he been thinking?

"I hope Mr. Harmless can get those emails."

"They may be nothing, Colin, totally unrelated to Amanda's...death."

"Anything out of the ordinary needs to be examined." He smacked his forehead. "I completely forgot."

"What?"

He shoved his hand into his pocket to dig out the chain he'd found in the basement at Columbella House. He dangled it from his finger. It was a bracelet.

"I found this in the basement right before you screamed bloody murder. Do you recognize it? Is it Amanda's?"

Michelle fingered the bracelet and the charms hanging from it. She plucked one charm out from the rest and squinted at it. Then she dropped her hand as if the charm had scorched her.

Chapter Six

Michelle rubbed the tips of her tingling fingers against the leg of her shorts, trying to erase memories.

"Is it Amanda's?" Colin cupped the charm bracelet in the palm of his hand.

"N-no."

"But you know the owner?"

Warmth flared in Michelle's cheeks. It's like the woman had come back to haunt her this summer. "It's my mom's."

"This is your mom's bracelet?" Colin hooked his index finger around the chain and dangled it in front of his face.

"It didn't belong to my mom. She made it."

"Oh." He dropped the bracelet next to the laptop, where it coiled like a snake. "She made jewelry?"

"Yeah. No big deal. She crafted the pieces at home and sold them to her friends and some of the teenaged girls."

"But it didn't belong to Amanda."

Michelle poked at the bracelet, a bit tarnished and forlorn. "There's a charm with the initials MS. I'm assuming it belongs to one of the St. Regis twins since they were both in and out of the house when they were last here."

"Mystery solved. I won't bother turning it over to the police today." He glanced at his watch. "Do you want to head to the police station now?"

"Sure. Do you have a car or do you want me to drive?"

She swept the bracelet into her hand and stuffed it into her pocket.

"I have a rental."

She hooked her thumbs in the pockets of her shorts where the bracelet burned against her leg. Maybe she should leave it here. She didn't need the constant reminder of her mother gouging her thigh. "You know, I never even asked you where you live now. Are you in San Francisco?"

"L.A., although I've been thinking of requesting a transfer to San Francisco. One of my buddies is with the Bureau up there. He's the one who first told me about Tiffany Gunderson's murder."

"The local cops realize now that you're not here in any official capacity."

"I know, but I still feel obliged to share my opinions with them—that the Gunderson and Frank murders are related, and I believe Amanda's death is tied to theirs. This is the same guy."

"But why? Does he plan to work his way through the entire Coral Cove class that graduated ten years ago? Does he have something against those particular women...or me?" She couldn't stop the goose pimples that rushed across her arms.

Colin must've noticed her shiver because he took a step forward and rubbed his knuckles along her skin. "That's what I'm here to find out, whether the local cops like it or not. My parents were friends with the Gundersons. I at least owe it to them."

Michelle practically purred at his touch. If the local cops didn't like Colin's presence in Coral Cove...she did.

Two hours later, Colin stepped onto the sidewalk outside the Coral Cove Police Station and squinted at the sky. The sun was staging a valiant attack against the stubborn marine layer, hurriedly pricking through the gray muck before it was time to sink into the ocean.

Settling his shoulders against the brick facade of the building, Colin crossed his arms and dug his heels into the sidewalk. The small-town cops hadn't appreciated his meddling. They'd found a smear of blood on the transient's sleeve and had closed the case before the blood analysis had come back from the lab.

They hadn't been interested in rose petals, class connections or class reunions. The summer tourist season loomed less than two weeks away, and the chief and the mayor wanted to make sure nothing more than the haze from the ocean was hanging over Coral Cove by the time the crowds staggered in from L.A. and San Francisco.

Michelle rounded the corner, accompanied by a pumped-up guy in jeans and a Coral Cove High School sweatshirt, and waved. After she'd had her turn with the police, she'd gone to the high school to collect an answer key for some quizzes she had to grade. Looked like she'd brought the mascot with her.

Colin pushed off the wall of the police station. Michelle had been holding up well under the shock of her friend's murder and her proximity to the killer. But Colin had sensed her busywork and interest in helping him investigate sprang from a desire to keep her sadness at bay. Whatever worked. God knows, he'd employed a million devices to hold his own sorrow at arm's length.

"That didn't take long." Her eyes sparkled above flushed cheeks. "Colin Roarke, this is Larry Brunswick. He's head of the math department."

Colin shook the man's hand. Brunswick looked familiar. Must've been teaching when he'd attended CCHS. "I don't think I had you for any classes, but I think you were teaching when I was in high school."

"I started at Coral Cove the year your brother, Kieran, was a senior. So I had the thrill of watching him play. Helluva quarterback."

Colin schooled his face into a bland smile. If he went off on Brunswick like he had with that other teacher, Michelle would have him pegged as a loose cannon. And her opinion of him mattered more than he cared to admit.

"Yeah, he was."

"Not that you weren't an amazing player yourself."

Colin held up his hands and twisted his lips into a grin. "I'm not looking for kudos. Kieran was the better athlete."

The better man.

Brunswick's eyes clouded as he drew his brows together. "They still haven't… I mean, is he still considered missing?"

"Yeah." Colin felt Michelle's sharp glance like a needle poking his flesh. He kept his gaze pinned to Brunswick's sympathetic face.

"That's rough." Brunswick adjusted the satchel on his shoulder. "And now this in Coral Cove, Amanda's murder, I mean. And practically on Michelle's doorstep. I hear they got the guy."

"Maybe." His training had taught him never to give away too much information…to anyone.

"I hope so. My wife, Nancy, is nervous." Brunswick clicked his tongue. "Glad I decided to clean out my desk today and ran into you at school, Michelle, and had that answer key you needed."

"You're a lifesaver. I didn't want to do all those quadratic equations myself to grade the quizzes."

"Anytime." He rolled his wrist and checked his watch. "I'd better hurry or I'm going to be late picking up my wife. Good to see you, Colin."

One quick wave and Brunswick was practically jogging

down the sidewalk. "Does his wife keep him on a short leash or what?"

"She's a judge's daughter, kind of a diva." Michelle studied his face, and he smiled to avoid her scrutiny, to mask any residual pain that might be marking his features. "Do you want to grab a late lunch, compare notes?"

"Yeah, let's compare notes."

He steered her toward his buddy's restaurant, Burgers and Brews, but she shook her head.

"I just can't, I just…that's where Amanda and I had dinner last night."

"I'm sorry. Stupid of me to suggest it."

"I know Bryan Sotelo's your friend. I hope the macabre association doesn't hurt his business."

"In my experience, it tends to help a business—curiosity seekers."

"Ugh. I don't get that." She pointed across the street. "The Great Earth is pretty good."

He grabbed his throat and stuck out his tongue. "I don't do vegetarian."

"They have burgers and brews over there, too. Don't worry. I won't force you to eat alfalfa sprouts."

Five minutes later they were ensconced at a corner table, and Colin was running his fingers down a short list of burgers. "The sweet potato fries sound good."

"They are." Michelle's menu covered her entire face and she had a white-knuckled grip on its edges.

Colin tapped a finger on the top of the plastic menu. "Are you okay in there?"

She inched the menu down so that her big, brown eyes appeared over the top. "Everyone's talking about the murder. I keep catching snippets of conversation, and people keep throwing me sidelong glances. Maybe I shouldn't be out."

"Stop." He clapped the menu closed with his hands and

she flinched. "Of course everyone's gossiping about the murder. It's a big deal for a small town. Remember when that girl disappeared a few years ago from the music festival? I even heard about that and I wasn't living here."

"I hate it." She dropped her lashes, where they created dark crescents on her cheeks. "The gossip."

"It's a small town. And you have every right to be out for lunch. It doesn't mean you mourn your friend any less."

She grabbed a napkin and bunched it up at her nose. "I'm going to miss Amanda. You have to catch her killer, Colin. Amanda needs justice. She deserves justice."

"Maybe the Coral Cove P.D. has already caught him."

She snorted and then blew her nose. "You don't believe that any more than I do."

"Did the chief tell you about the blood on Chris's shirt?"

"Huh?"

The waitress interrupted to take their orders, and as she scribbled her shorthand on her pad, she glanced up at Michelle. "I'm really sorry about Amanda. I know you two were friends and you were right there when it happened."

"Thanks."

"You take care of yourself."

"See?" Colin touched the rim of his water glass to hers. "Nobody is blaming you or thinking you're weird because you're eating lunch."

She blew out a breath and took a sip of water. "Who's Chris?"

"Chief Evans didn't tell you?" The cops who'd questioned him hadn't exactly told him to keep mum about anything. He didn't owe them, anyway. He owed Michelle. "Chris Jeffers is the name of the transient. He had a smear of blood on his sleeve."

"Amanda's?" Her eyes widened.

"They don't know yet. They sent it out for testing and depending on how backed up the lab is, it could take a while for them to get the results."

"But it's something. Maybe you're wrong, Colin." She shot him an apologetic look from beneath her lashes. "Maybe Amanda's murder was just a random act. I'm not saying the other two murders, Tiffany's and Belinda's, are random, but maybe Amanda's death has nothing to do with those other women."

His gut rebelled against her reasoning. Three women from the same high school class? Two with slit throats and all with rose petals? But his heart softened when he saw the hope shining in Michelle's eyes.

She wanted to believe Amanda's murder was a random act of violence. She wanted to believe she had nothing to fear from the same killer. And he didn't want to dash that belief. Not now.

"Maybe." He shoved their water glasses aside as the waitress brought their plates. "Now let me see if they snuck any alfalfa sprouts on my burger."

Pointing to her salad, she said, "You can toss them on here if you find any."

They ate in silence for several minutes, and then Michelle started shoving lettuce leaves around her plate.

"What's wrong? Tired of rabbit food?"

"How's the burger? Not too healthy for you?"

Chewing, he raised his eyes to the ceiling. "Just the right amount of grease. And these sweet potato fries are great. Have one."

She picked a fry from his plate and twirled it around. "Colin. What happened to your brother in Afghanistan?"

He nearly choked on his water. *Damn.* He thought he'd escaped the inquisition. He blotted his mouth with a napkin, stalling for time. Of course he could take his usual route—stare down the questioner and grunt. But Michelle wasn't some random nosy person on the street. She'd opened up to him about her past hurts and now she'd volleyed the ball into his court.

Isn't that how relationships worked? Give and take. Not that he and Michelle had a relationship. They had more like a partnership. He'd keep her safe and she'd feed him information about her graduating class at CCHS.

Did he have to open up to a partner?

"Of course, you don't have to talk about it if you don't want to." She dropped the sweet potato fry onto her half-eaten salad and brushed her fingers together.

His eyes met hers. Tiny creases marred the smooth skin between her dark, sculpted eyebrows. She looked worried... worried about him.

He scooped in a breath and twisted the napkin in his lap. "My brother and I were both on the same intelligence-gathering team. We'd been watching a particular bunch outside of Kandahar. We made our move, but someone had betrayed us. They were ready for us."

"What happened?"

"The Taliban killed a few of the team members and captured the rest of us, including me and Kieran."

"I—I had heard something about that, later when you escaped."

Colin's heart hammered in his chest. He could never get past this part of the story with anyone, not even in his own mind. "I escaped. But Kieran didn't. We'd planned our escape, but our captors chose that night to take Kieran away for questioning. I wanted to stay, but they had talked about moving us to a different location. The others convinced me, but I should've held out. I should've stayed with my brother."

"Of course you couldn't have stayed." Her hand inched closer to his and then froze as his fingers curled into a fist.

"Is he dead?"

"No." Colin smacked his clenched hand table. "After we escaped, we went back for him, but, of course, the Taliban had pulled up stakes and moved on."

"And you never..." Her fingers nervously pleated the tablecloth.

"We never found Kieran's body. That's why I still hold out hope that he's alive somewhere."

"You blame yourself."

That about summed it up. His lips twisted into a grimace. "Kieran never would've left me behind, Michelle."

"You don't know that." She skimmed her fingers along the scars on his wrists. "He would've done what was best for the whole team, right? Just as you did."

Her light touch calmed the blood thrumming through his veins. He felt...unburdened. And that wasn't fair. Michelle had her own turmoil to deal with right now.

"I'm sorry." Closing his eyes, he pinched the bridge of his nose.

"Don't be. I asked. I wanted to know. If we're going to work together on this thing, I want you to trust me."

He opened one eye. "We're working together in the loosest sense of that term. I ask you questions about your classmates and you provide the answers. No more traipsing around haunted houses."

She flipped her hair over her shoulder in a sassy move that made his stomach flip with it. "That haunted house may have given up Amanda's killer. I'm not giving up hope that Chris is our guy. I guess we'll know when the blood test comes back."

"Maybe our partnership will come to an end sooner rather than later, which would be a good thing." *Good for Michelle's safety, anyway.*

She nodded. "Absolutely. Of course, if this guy Chris is

arrested for Amanda's murder, it doesn't solve the other two murders."

"We'll let the FBI agents assigned to those cases worry about that." He signaled to the waitress. "You probably have to get home and grade those quizzes."

"Yeah, just another exciting Saturday night."

She made a grab for the check, but he beat her to it. "Are you looking for excitement? I would've thought you'd had your fill."

Her cheeks burned red. "I didn't mean that. Amanda's been dead for less than twenty-four hours. The last thing I need is excitement."

Colin grabbed her hand and gave it a squeeze. "Don't feel guilty for surviving."

"Like you do?"

"That's…different."

"If you say so." She tilted her chin at the check on the table. "How much do I owe?"

"It's on me. You can get the next one." Because he really wanted there to be a next one.

The sun had made its brief appearance. Now the marine layer was staging a comeback. Michelle peered at the sky through the windshield of her car.

"It's going to be another one of those nights." Her fingers white-knuckled the steering wheel.

"Are you going to be okay?"

"Sure. The chief said he'd send a patrol car by the house a few times tonight."

"And I'm right down the street."

"I'll keep that in mind, but unless you remember quadratic equations, I think I can handle things."

If she asked him to stay he'd accept in a heartbeat, but Michelle had an independent streak and he had to respect that. Who knows? Maybe after he'd told her how he'd left

Kieran to fend for himself, she didn't trust him to protect her. Hell, he wouldn't.

She slowed the car as she approached her house. "Do you want a lift to your place?"

"I can walk."

She swung into her driveway, avoiding the bedraggled yellow tape from the crime scene, and Colin reached into his pocket for a card.

"Do you still have my card from last night?"

"I think it's in my purse."

He pressed another one into her palm. "Here it is again, just in case. My cell phone number is on there. Call me if... if you need anything."

Her doe eyes searched his face, and he relaxed the muscles and even managed a smile. He didn't want to scare her.

"Thanks, Colin. I think I'll be okay. After grading, I'm going to bed early. I didn't sleep well last night."

"Sounds like a good idea." He walked her to the front door, and she gave him a tremulous smile and slipped inside.

He strolled to the end of her walkway and shoved his hands in his pockets as he stared at the spot where Amanda had been killed. He knew that homeless guy wasn't responsible for the murder. When would the police realize it? When the killer cut down another member of Michelle's graduating class?

He turned and surveyed Michelle's tidy beach house through half-closed lids. Michelle was not going to be the next victim. And he'd make damned sure of it.

He had no intention of running away...this time.

Several hours later, Michelle stretched and dropped her red pen on the coffee table where she'd been grading the algebra quizzes. She'd planned on getting them done early, having a light dinner and then turning in, but the hands on her watch were creeping toward midnight.

She hadn't been able to focus all night. Or rather she hadn't been able to focus on algebra all night. Her thoughts had drifted down the street toward Colin Roarke. No wonder he'd seemed sad that first night she'd seen him. He'd left his brother behind. Had escaped while his brother faced an uncertain future—maybe death.

She'd wanted to assuage his guilt, but she hadn't been very successful. It was easy to tell other people to shrug off their guilt. Outsiders had a more logical, more clinical approach to someone else's situation. After what had happened to Amanda, Michelle found it easy to understand Colin's feelings.

Would she always feel this way? Would she always wonder if there was something more she could've done for Amanda? Maybe she should've insisted that Amanda spend the night.

Michelle crossed the room to the window and lifted the side of the curtains. The weather outside mimicked the conditions of last night and she gave an involuntary shiver. The fog had rolled in thick and heavy, blanketing the street in its moist embrace.

Clutching her upper arms, Michelle balanced a shoulder against the wall. She'd already spotted one cop car on a drive-by. She'd be fine. Except now she couldn't discern a cop car on the street even if it drove by with flashing lights. And the cop couldn't see her.

Michelle let the curtain fall, tousled her hair and yawned. She stuffed the last of the quizzes into the folder for that class and glanced at her laptop. Should she enter the grades online tonight or wait until tomorrow?

She plopped the folders on top of the closed laptop and spun around. She'd wait until tomorrow when her eyelids didn't have to be propped open with toothpicks.

She turned off the light in the living room and clicked on

the lamp by her bed. She peeled off her clothes, tossed them in the basket in her closet and padded to the attached bathroom in her bra and undies.

Still unable to get Colin off her mind, she brushed her teeth and scrubbed her skin as if that could expunge the image of his face imprinted on her brain. She didn't need to renew her schoolgirl crush on Colin Roarke. He'd be moving on soon enough.

She wandered back into the bedroom, massaging night cream into her face. She slipped out of her bra and tugged a long T-shirt over her head that had Math Teachers Do It With Pi emblazoned across the front—a silly gift from Amanda. Kicking off her flip-flops, she reached for the lamp.

She froze.

She'd heard a scratching sound on the window like a twig scraping the glass. Only she didn't have any trees outside her bedroom window.

She held her breath. She squinted at the filmy white curtains. It could just be grains of sand whipped up from the sand dunes.

With her heart pounding, she sidled along the wall toward the window. Crouching down, she inched the curtain to the side. A wave of fear rushed through every cell of her body as she watched a hand scrabble at her window.

Chapter Seven

Michelle screamed and tumbled to the floor. Her fingers had curled around the curtains, and they ripped as she brought them down with her.

Still clutching a piece of white linen in her fist, she scrambled toward the bedroom door on her hands and knees. She glanced over her shoulder at the gaping rip in the curtains framing a smooth expanse of glass. No face. No hand.

Had she imagined it, that hand clawing at the windowpane?

Someone yelled and pounded on her front door. Michelle let out another yelp. She leaped to her feet and dashed for her cell phone, charging on the kitchen counter.

"Michelle!" Another bang on the door. "Michelle! It's Colin."

The phone slipped through her grasp as relief surged through her body. She peeked through the peephole and sagged against the door. With shaky fingers she turned the dead bolt and swung open the door.

Colin charged over the threshold and Michelle didn't know if he'd swept her into his arms or if she'd fallen there, but here she was tucked against his solid chest.

"I heard you scream, what happened? Are you okay?"

He'd heard her scream from down the block?

She took a ragged breath that scorched her lungs. Maybe

her scream *had* carried all the way to his house. "I—I saw something at the window."

"What window? Not the front?"

"My bedroom window."

His arms tightened around her. "A face?"

"A hand." A tremble rolled through her, and his embrace got tighter.

"You saw a hand at your bedroom window? Trying to open the window? Trying to break it?"

"I don't know. Maybe pressed against the pane, scratching at the glass."

He kicked the door shut behind him and advanced into the room with her still clinging to his neck. "Show me."

She untwined her arms and stepped back. She'd never been the clingy type before, but his strong arms had offered an oasis she couldn't resist.

Time to buck up and be a math teacher.

She pointed to her abbreviated hallway. "My bedroom's back here."

He followed her into the room, and she tugged on the hem of her T-shirt, for the first time realizing she was dressed for bed…or underdressed. Then she remembered the wording on the front of her T-shirt, and she crossed her arms over her chest.

"Whoa! What happened to the curtains?"

"I did that." She gestured toward the piece of curtain she'd abandoned near the bedroom door. "I had it in my hand when I stumbled backward."

Colin prowled toward the window and yanked back the bedraggled curtains.

Michelle jumped.

He raised a brow. "Okay, what did you see?"

"I was just about to turn off the lamp on my nightstand, and I heard a scratching sound at the window."

"Trees or bushes out there?"

"No. Sand dunes."

"So you went to the window to check it out?"

"Well, I sort of peered out, and that's when I saw the hand."

"And the person attached to this hand wasn't trying to open the window or break it?"

"Not that I could see. It was weird. It was like a disembodied hand. I didn't see anything else."

"The guy could've been crouched below the window, reaching up."

Michelle sucked in her lower lip. "Or maybe there was no hand or no body attached to the hand. Maybe I imagined it."

"Do you really believe that?"

"I don't know. After I screamed and headed for the door, I looked and there was nothing there."

"He heard you and took off. Believe me, that was some scream."

"How did you hear me? How did you get here?"

A red flush crept across his face. "I…uh…was outside your house. Your scream carried outside the house, or at least I thought I heard something. And when I looked at your house, I could see the lights still on."

He'd been outside her house? "Why… What…?"

"I couldn't sleep. I went out to chuck rocks at the water. Since I hadn't seen a patrol car since I'd been outside, I decided to cruise past your house myself."

"I'm glad you did. The hand freaked me out."

"So now you did see a hand."

Shaking her head, she shoved her hair behind one ear. "I don't know, Colin."

"Do you want to call the police?"

"I was on my way to do just that when you started pounding on my door. Do you think it's worth it now? If there was someone outside my window, he's long gone."

He shrugged. "They can dust for prints."

Her gaze swept Colin's reassuringly large frame. He offered the only protection she needed.

"Do you think a murderer is going to leave his fingerprints on windowpanes?"

"Nope, but an even better argument against calling the local police is that I'd like to check the area around your window myself tomorrow morning. And I'd like to do it before some officer of the law tramps around out there."

"That settles it then. I'd rather have you looking out there than the cops who are already happy with their suspect."

Colin rubbed the gauzy material of the curtains between his fingers. "You need thicker curtains at your window."

"There's nothing on the other side except the dunes, and I have a fence separating my yard from the dunes."

"Don't the teenagers still hang out in the sand dunes?"

"Once in a while, but they don't venture into my yard."

"Maybe they did tonight." He drummed his fingers against the window. "Do you have a sheet or something you can hang over this window?"

Michelle gave him a sheet from the linen closet and he draped it over the curtain rod, covering the window and the torn curtains.

"Thanks, Colin. I'm glad you were…taking a walk."

"Me, too, but I hope that's not your way of kicking me out of your house."

"It must be past 1:00 a.m."

"Must be. But if you think I'm leaving you here alone with disembodied hands at the window and see-through curtains, you're crazy."

A warm rush of…something sweet coursed through her veins. "I'm a mathematician. I'm too logical to be crazy."

"Except maybe crazy about pi."

She glanced down at her sleep shirt, her cheeks warming. "Oh, this silly thing."

"I like it." His blue eyes glowed with an inner fire that singed the ends of her lashes. "I like it a lot."

She giggled. No, she laughed, because Michelle Girard *never* giggled. Then she ducked her head in the linen closet again. "I'll get you a blanket and pillow for the couch. Unless you'd rather have a sleeping bag for the floor."

"I'd rather— The couch will be fine."

She held out the blanket and pillow for him, and he took them from her, grazing her arm with his hand. She held herself erect, as an overwhelming desire to throw herself against his chest again surged through her body.

He dumped the blanket onto the couch. "Leave your door open just in case. And if you see or hear anything, don't hesitate to let loose with one of those screams."

"Okay, I can do that." She added a chipper note to her voice to defuse the double entendre. Or was she the only one thinking about a different kind of scream?

Michelle left her door halfway open and crawled into bed, her gaze darting to the makeshift curtain across the window. Had she imagined the hand?

She pulled the pillow to her chest and buried her face into its softness. Whether the hand was real or not, it had brought Colin to her doorstep. And he brought safety and security.

Or maybe he brought more danger than she could handle.

COLIN WIGGLED HIS TOES against the chill seeping into his feet. His nostrils twitched at the smell of rich coffee wafting through the air. *Heaven.*

He shifted on the uncomfortable couch and peeled open one eye. Michelle buzzed around the kitchen, clinking dishes and dipping in and out of the refrigerator. *Pure heaven.*

He'd had an uneasy feeling last night ever since he'd left Michelle at her front door after their late lunch. The cops were complacent. That was a bad state of mind—especially for a cop.

He'd noticed the patrol car of one of Coral Cove's finest cruising down the street once or twice, but Michelle needed more than that. He couldn't sleep, anyway, and tossing rocks into the inky ocean seemed like a logical alternative. Once outside, his feet beat an automatic path to Michelle's house.

He'd been on high alert, his ears attuned to the slightest sound. He hadn't even been sure the noise he'd heard had been a scream or that it had come from Michelle's house. But it was all the signal he'd needed.

"Did I wake you?"

He blinked and the vision in the kitchen came into focus. "The smell of that coffee woke me up. I know you don't drink the stuff. You didn't have to go through any trouble for me."

"My dad was a coffee drinker, and I still have the coffee-maker—no trouble at all. Besides, it's the least I can do for a midnight rescue. Black, right?"

She poured a cup of the steaming brew and carried it to him along with a sliced bagel on a plate. She'd already showered and changed from her sexy nightshirt with the sexy slogan into a pair of cargo shorts, a T-shirt and a light sweatshirt to ward off the nip in the morning air.

"Do you want some cream cheese with your bagel?"

"Sure." He swung his legs over the side of the couch, clutching the blanket in his lap. He'd shed his jeans last night and hadn't expected breakfast in bed this morning. Not that he minded.

She placed the coffee cup and bagel on the coffee table and retreated to the kitchen for the cream cheese. As she approached him, her gaze dropped to his bare chest. Her cheeks blanched and she averted her eyes.

"Here you go." She settled the tub of cream cheese with a knife crossed over the top next to the plate.

Before she could draw away, he encircled her wrist with two fingers. "A lovely parting gift from my captors."

She dropped her lashes. "What'd they do?"

He ran a finger along one of the scars crisscrossing his chest. "You don't want to know."

"I'm sorry, even though that's pretty inadequate."

"It's adequate." He released her and peeled the lid from the cream cheese container. He spread a thick layer on a toasted bagel half. "Are you joining me or did you already eat?"

"I already had something." She jerked her thumb over her shoulder. "Are we going outside when you finish?"

"Yeah. Have you looked out there yet?"

"I looked out the window and didn't see a thing. Just sand."

Several minutes later, Colin finished off his bagel and took a last gulp of coffee. While Michelle carried the dishes back to the kitchen, he let the blanket slip to the floor and snagged his jeans from the back of the couch.

She walked back into the room as he was yanking his pants over his thighs. Pink suffused her cheeks, and he couldn't help grinning as he zipped his fly. Despite the veneer of sophistication she wore, Michelle wasn't much different from that bashful high school girl with the endless legs and silver in her mouth.

"Are you coming with me?"

"Of course."

He shrugged into his sweatshirt and shoved his weapon in the pocket. In response to her raised eyebrows, he said, "In case the hand makes an appearance."

She led him through a side door in the kitchen and he stepped off the concrete porch behind her. The back of her house abutted the sand dunes, just like his. The houses across the street from theirs, like Columbella House, had the ocean tumbling away from their backyards. They just had mountains of sand.

Her backyard was accessible from the front with not even a fence between them. "Anyone off the street can get into your backyard."

"Yeah, well, I never had to worry about that before."

They turned the corner of her small beach cottage where two windows faced the sand dunes. She pointed to first one and then the other. "Those are both bedrooms. The first one is mine."

Colin eyed the bottoms of the windows, which reached about waist-high. Anyone could climb through those windows. Before he clumped through the sand to the window, he asked, "I suppose you wouldn't notice any footprints out of the ordinary back here, would you?"

Michelle looked down at the bumps and indentations in the sand and shook her head. "You can't really make out footprints in dry sand, can you?"

"Not really." He shuffled through the sand and crouched beside her window. "If you saw a disembodied hand, it's because the hand's owner was down here. You couldn't see the rest of his body or his face because he was hiding below the window and reaching up with his hand."

"Why would he do that if he were trying to break in or even peer through the window like a Peeping Tom?" She hugged herself and hunched her shoulders.

"Maybe he thought he could cut the glass first before reaching in to unlock the slider."

She shook her head and her light brown hair slipped over her shoulder. "I'm pretty sure he wasn't holding a glass-cutting tool. He was scratching or almost clawing at the window."

Colin mumbled more to himself than Michelle. "Why would you scratch at a window?"

"Huh?"

He ignored her question and brushed his fingers on the front of his sweatshirt, the muscle in his jaw jumping. He smoothed the tips of his fingers across the glass in a grid pattern—up and down and left to right. Then he moved on to the next quarter of the window. He sucked in a breath.

"What is it?"

Lightly, he traced the pads of his fingers over the rough spot on the windowpane. With his nose almost touching the glass, he scraped at the patch with his fingernail.

He held up his finger, dug the residue from beneath his fingernail with his other nail and rubbed the sticky substance between his thumb and forefinger.

"Colin, what did you find? Looks like a grain of sand to me, which wouldn't be all that unusual."

She'd crouched down beside him, and he extended his finger beneath her nose. "It's adhesive."

"Adhesive? You mean like tape?"

"Yeah, or more likely one of those two-sided adhesive strips."

Her eyes widened and he could see flecks of gold in her irises. "What does that mean? I've never taped anything to the outside of this window."

"I didn't figure you had, which means someone else did."

"How old is that stuff? It could've been my dad."

He rolled the adhesive between his fingers. "It's still sticky. Old stuff wouldn't be sticky anymore, or it would be covered with sand. This isn't."

"I don't get it, Colin." A note of panic had crept into her

voice and he cursed himself for being the one to keep bringing bad news into her life.

"Help me search the ground." He tapped the window to replace the adhesive and dropped to his hands and knees. Michelle liked to keep active, to be involved.

"Wh-what are we looking for?"

"Anything out of the ordinary. A button. A cigarette butt. A chewing gum wrapper."

She skimmed her hands across the sand, sifting her fingers through the silvery grains. "A button?"

"A button?" Colin sat back on his heels.

Michelle held out her cupped hand to him. "Not a button like from someone's shirt, but a black button that looks like it could've broken off some machinery or something."

Colin's heart jumped in his chest as he held out a surprisingly steady hand to receive Michelle's discovery.

She turned her hand over, dumping the object into his waiting palm.

He wedged the black disc between two fingers and brought it close to his face. He ran the pad of his finger along the smooth side of the disc, but it wasn't so smooth.

The same sticky substance he'd collected from the window was present on the disc. He closed his fist around the button and cursed, a black fury beating wings in his chest.

Michelle dug her fingers into the sand. "What is it?"

Colin drew in a steadying breath to keep from smashing his fist into the wall of Michelle's house.

"It's a camera."

Chapter Eight

Pinpricks of shock raced along Michelle's flesh. And then she laughed. "A camera? That little thing?"

But Colin didn't get the joke.

He opened his hand and the black device in the middle of his palm stared at her, like an evil eye.

Her smile collapsed. "Tell me you're kidding."

"It's a spy camera, but you don't have to be James Bond to get one. Anyone can order one of these off the internet."

"And what's it doing on the ground outside my bedroom window?" She pressed her hand over her heart as if she could rein in its wild gallop.

Colin flipped the button over with his thumbnail. "It's sticky on this side, just like the adhesive from your windowpane. Someone stuck this—" he held it up "—onto your window."

Michelle tried to swallow, but her dry throat wouldn't cooperate. "D-do you think that's what he was trying to do last night? Place the camera?"

"Place it or retrieve it."

"Once in place, why would he try to take it back?"

"The chips in these cameras are set to record for only so many hours." He slipped the camera into the pocket of his sweatshirt. "Once the time is up, you have to retrieve them to download your recording."

"Recording? Like a video camera?" The hair on the back of her neck stood at attention, and she had to grind her teeth to keep them from chattering.

"Yeah, it's a video camera, Michelle." They'd been squatting in the sand, and now Colin rose, hooking his hand beneath her arm.

Her knees quaked and she wedged her shoulder against the stucco wall of her house. Someone had been spying on her. Before she examined the why, she wanted to know the how. The how would make her feel more in control, make her take a detour from the land of feelings to the land of reason…and action.

"How does it work? How can something so small do so much work?"

The harsh lines around Colin's mouth softened. "It's those tiny computer chips. The device is remotely controlled. You can hook it up to your computer and download the video. This one looks like it needs a special attachment and maybe some special software."

"That's amazing." And knowledge was power. She pushed off the wall and squared her shoulders.

"I'm sure you've heard about cases where these spy cameras were installed in women's dressing rooms or bathrooms. The women don't even notice them."

"Do you know how to download the video?"

"If I had the right stuff on my PC, I could figure it out. But I have a better idea."

"The police?" The wobblies came back in full force as Michelle thought about the cops on the Coral Cove P.D. watching video of her coming and going from her bedroom to her bathroom.

"Too slow. Too much bureaucracy." He took her hand and pulled her away from the side of the house. "I have a buddy in the county sheriff's department. Played football with him in high school. He does this sort of thing all the time."

"How soon could he find out what's on that thing?"

"I made him look really good on the football field. If I get the camera to him this morning, he might be able to get us a read by the end of the day."

Michelle stumbled as she rounded the corner to her front yard and Colin caught her just as he'd done every time since he'd entered her life two days ago.

"Will your friend be able to tell anything about the person who planted the camera?"

"Before I realized what it was, I had my fingers all over the surfaces. Even if the perpetrator had left any prints, which I doubt he did, I pretty much destroyed them. If we can nail down the make and model, we could start tracing that way, but there are a lot of these things around."

"Do you think it's him, Colin? Do you think it was the killer who planted the camera and then returned to my house to retrieve it?"

"I don't know, sweetheart, but it would be really interesting to find out if Amanda had one of these stuck to her window."

"We'll have to find out, won't we?" She charged up the front steps and held open the door for him.

He stopped and wedged a knuckle beneath her chin. "Feel okay now?"

"I'll feel a lot better when we nail this sicko."

Colin grinned and dropped a kiss on the top of her head. "That's my girl."

Despite the ball of fear lodged in her gut, Michelle floated into the house on wisps of hope. Had Colin Roarke just called her *sweetheart* and *his girl* in the space of two minutes?

She felt like a high school girl who'd just gotten a letterman's jacket from the star football player. Only she'd gotten something much more important than a jacket from this star football player—she'd gotten consideration and admiration. And that was better than being a cheerleader and homecoming queen all wrapped up in one.

COLIN LANDED ON HER DOORSTEP five hours later with good news. "I dropped off the camera with my buddy Jake Powell. He's working a case today, but he thinks he can get to our little project by the end of the day."

"Jake Powell." Michelle bit her lower lip. "That name sounds familiar."

"I told you he went to CCHS. Since he's a year older than I am, he was already out of school when you were a freshman."

"Did you tell him it was me? That I might be starring in those images?"

"Of course. He knows you were the last one to see Amanda alive, and that the murder took place on the street in front of your house." He squeezed her shoulder. "Don't worry. Jake's totally professional."

She lifted one eyebrow. "If he's so professional, did he ask you why you were using him instead of turning the device over to the Coral Cove P.D. or someone in his department working on the case?"

"Touché." He shoved his hands in his pockets and hunched his shoulders. "In our line of work, we know when to ask questions and when to zip it."

She dragged her gaze away from the way his jeans tightened when he had his hands bunched in his pockets. She'd spent most of this Sunday afternoon cleaning house and trying to sweep away thoughts of Colin from her mind. She understood her attraction to him. Schoolgirl crushes died hard. But she'd had a harder time figuring out why his blue eyes smoldered when he looked at her or why his hands always reached for her.

Must be that protective instinct.

She cleared her throat. "Are we going to Amanda's house now?"

"Good, you waited for me. I was afraid you'd traipse over there on your own."

"Me, poke around a house that someone may be watching? The same someone who's been watching me? No, thanks."

"I knew you were smart." He touched his finger to her nose.

She grabbed a sweatshirt from the hook by the door because from the look of things, the sun wouldn't be out much longer.

As she pulled the door closed, Colin snapped his fingers. "Amanda's husband might have moved back into the house. Didn't you tell me he moved out during the separation?"

"He's staying at his parents' place." She dangled her keys. "The house is on the other side of town in that new development."

On the drive to Amanda's house, Michelle asked about the case against the transient. She was still holding out hope that the police had caught the killer, but she shared Colin's gut instinct that the cops had the wrong guy.

"Did the P.D. get anything more on Chris the homeless guy?"

"Nope. I think old Chris is enjoying his three hots and a cot right now. I don't think he's too concerned, since he knows he's innocent…unless the cops try to railroad him."

"They wouldn't do that. I know Chief Evans wants Amanda's murder solved before the summer tourist season, but he doesn't have anything to prove. I heard he's applying to a few big-city departments, so he probably won't be around much longer, anyway."

After driving through downtown Coral Cove, Michelle took a street that wound into the low-lying hills tucked against Coral Cove's eastern border.

Colin whistled. "These are some nice houses up here, but I still like our side of town better."

"They definitely get more sunshine up here." Her car rolled along newish streets that formed a neat crisscross pattern. When she rounded the corner of Amanda's street, she swallowed hard.

How many times had she visited Amanda up here? That night Amanda should've reconciled with Ryan, and the two of them would've come back here to make up.

She suppressed a shiver. Amanda had never suspected a thing. Or had she? Had someone been sending her faintly disturbing emails? Had someone left rose petals for her? Had she been hearing noises outside her window?

If so, she'd never mentioned anything to Michelle.

She pulled alongside a curb several houses down from Amanda's. She pointed. "That's her house, seven twenty-two."

"Why are we parked here?"

"I don't know. I don't want to look suspicious." Her cheeks heated up under Colin's eyes shining with humor. "You know. Maybe someone's watching."

He nodded briskly. "Good idea."

A couple of kids riding scooters in the street stopped to stare at them, but beyond that audience, Michelle and Colin slipped through the gate leading to Amanda's backyard unnoticed.

"Do you know which one is her bedroom window?"

"It's at the end."

They crossed the small yard, a little overgrown since

Obsession

Ryan's absence from the house. Michelle stopped in front of the last set of windows. "There's another window around the corner of the house."

"Okay. Let's check here first." Colin wiped his hands across the soft cotton covering his stomach. Then he trailed his fingers along the glass of the window, carefully outlining a grid pattern like he had done on her window.

"I don't feel anything. You want to check around on the ground?"

"I don't think we're going to get lucky twice." She crouched down and scanned the ground below Amanda's window. An object like that little camera would jump right out at her on this light-colored cement.

"Nothing. You?" Colin brushed his long fingers together with a frown creasing his forehead.

"No. Let's try the other window."

They turned the corner to the side of the house. "This is another bedroom window and the small one farther down is the bathroom."

She gritted her teeth against the sour taste that rose from her belly when she thought about someone recording her every move in her own bedroom.

Colin rubbed his hands together before continuing his examination of the surface of the window, like a blind man reading Braille.

Michelle couldn't help the thought that slammed into her brain—*what would those fingers feel like trailing along the bare skin of her body?*

She dropped to her knees and combed through the dirt in the flower bed beneath the window. No roses here, just neglected impatiens. Ryan had been the one with the green thumb.

Now Amanda was as dead as those flowers.

"There's nothing here, Michelle. No trace evidence of any adhesive on these windows, no camera."

She flicked a dried leaf from a drooping flower. "If this is the same guy, why would he change his mode of operation? Why watch me when he never watched Amanda?"

"We don't know that he never watched Amanda. We can't find any evidence he did, but that doesn't mean much."

"Nothing means much, including that transient hiding out at Columbella House."

He grazed the top of her head with his knuckles, and then dropped to his haunches beside her. "I thought you were halfway to believing the cops had their man."

"I was hoping…until we found that camera at my place. No way a guy like Chris would have the means to buy a device like that."

"Maybe the camera is unrelated to the murder."

She puffed at a strand of hair sticking to the lip balm on her lips. "Not likely."

"Who knows?" He took her arm and pulled her up as he straightened to his full height. "Maybe it's a horny student hoping to catch a glimpse of his hot algebra teacher."

Michelle stiffened. *Like mother, like daughter?*

Colin swore under his breath. "I'm an idiot, Michelle. I didn't mean…"

She held up a dirt-smudged hand. "It's okay. My mom wasn't even a teacher."

He placed his palm against hers, dwarfing her hand. "Enough sleuthing for the day. While we're waiting around for Jake's call, I'm going to take you out to dinner…after you wash your hands."

She slid her hand from his and wiped it on the seat of her denim shorts. "You took me out to dinner last night."

"Technically, that was lunch. I haven't been to Neptune's

Catch since I've been back." He nudged her toward the front of Amanda's house, and she didn't resist.

"Neptune's Catch is an overpriced tourist trap."

"Yeah, but it has great calamari, the best view in town— and my friend's family owns it."

"Oops, no offence to your friend's family." She stopped on the sidewalk and clicked the remote for the car. "Are you personal friends with all the restaurateurs in town?"

"Not the owners of that vegetarian place yesterday." He came around and opened the driver's-side door for her. "So what do you say? Neptune's at six o'clock so we can get a good table for the sunset?"

She leaned against the car. Did he think he had to babysit her? Should she let him? She chewed her lip, fighting back her old insecurities.

"If I hear from Jake before then, I'll let you know."

Is that what he thought she was worried about? It was probably what she *should* be worried about instead of trying to second-guess Colin's motives.

"Okay. I finished grading all the quizzes yesterday, so I'm free."

"Great." He slammed the car door.

Michelle watched him going around to the passenger side of the car in the rearview mirror. She wanted to be with Colin. Wanted to spend every minute he had left in town with him.

And her desire had nothing to do with fear…and everything to do with making good on her hot teenage crush.

COLIN STEERED AROUND the crime scene in front of Michelle's house. The cops hadn't been out here all day, so they must be done with it. Soon they'd remove the barriers and the yellow tape, and the only reminder of Amanda's murder would be a stain on the road.

And the hole it had carved in Michelle's belly.

He checked his cell phone for about the tenth time in the past hour. He'd left two messages for Jake, but he hadn't gotten back to him yet. Maybe there had been nothing to download from the camera. The guy could've been trying to hook it up when Michelle interrupted him.

He swung through the little gate that offered no protection to Michelle's house and knocked on her door. She opened the door a sliver and then swung it open.

He swallowed. A flowery dress skimmed Michelle's long, lean lines. She had on low heels, but it didn't matter. Even if she'd worn sky-high stilettos, she still couldn't match his height. Her light brown hair, the color of caramel or peanut brittle, something definitely sweet, brushed her shoulders, catching the light from the porch bulb above.

"You look pretty."

She got prettier when a hint of rose brushed her cheeks. "Thanks. It's just about the dressiest place in Coral Cove, so I figured I'd better at least wash the dirt from my hands and knees."

"Looks like you did a lot more than that." He gestured to his car parked behind hers in the driveway. "Are you ready?"

"Let me grab my purse and sweater," she called back over her shoulder. "Have you heard anything from Jake yet?"

"Not a word. I left him a message and told him to text me if he had anything."

They drove down the coast to the more touristy area of Coral Cove. Jagged rocks and rugged coastline punctuated the ocean on their end of town, which smoothed into wide, sandy beaches on the south end. Hotels and rental cottages dotted the road winding past the beaches, and several chain restaurants had sprung up in his absence.

Neptune's Catch had a prime spot situated on a hill overlooking the beach with a gentle path down to the sand. They took advantage of their position with an outdoor patio with several heat lamps to warm the chilly nights.

Michelle opted for a table on the half-empty patio. In a few weeks, this place would be packed. As they followed the hostess to their table, they almost collided with another couple coming from the bar.

"Excuse us." Colin placed his hand on Michelle's back to steer her around the other people. He felt her muscles tighten beneath his touch.

"Hello, Michelle." The slightly stooped man stretched his lips into a smile as if afraid a bigger one might split his face.

"Hello, Bob." She nodded to the woman beside him. "Marybeth."

Marybeth looked about ready to blow a gasket. She sniffed, her patrician nose flaring at the nostrils. Then, without a word to Michelle, she grabbed her milquetoast husband's arm and yanked him in her wake. To his credit, he managed a weak wave without his wife's noticing.

Their hostess turned, her vapid smile not registering anything other than a desire to return to the hostess stand. "Here's your table. Your waiter will be with you shortly. Enjoy your dinner."

Colin pulled out Michelle's chair, and she sat down stiffly. He dropped in the chair across from her and tilted his chin toward the bar. "What was that all about? Who were those lovely people?"

"That was Bob and Marybeth Hastings."

He raised his eyebrows. The names meant nothing to him, but obviously they meant a lot to Michelle, since she'd pronounced the names like an oracle of doom. "And they are… the local tax collectors? The overseers of all math teachers?"

She grimaced, not quite getting into the spirit of his humor. "They are the parents of Eric Hastings."

The lightbulb went on. "Ah, the young man who fell under your mother's spell."

"Yep."

A busboy dropped off a couple of glasses of water, and Michelle downed half of hers in one gulp.

"Well, Mr. Hastings doesn't seem to despise you, anyway."

She tracked squiggles on the sweating glass of ice water. "He's gotten over it, but she never will."

"She can't seriously blame you for your mom's actions?"

"I don't think she blames me. I'm just a reminder."

"Do you mind if I ask you whatever became of that… relationship?"

"I think they actually stayed together for a few years, probably felt they had to after devastating so many lives. Then they went their separate ways."

"You're not in touch with your mom?"

"No."

Her *no* shut the door on further questioning, and he didn't blame her. When people probed him about Kieran, he felt like punching them in the face. Except Michelle. Somehow he hadn't minded telling her about what had happened.

Their waiter introduced himself like he was their best friend and reeled off the evening's specials. Since Michelle didn't drink, Colin ordered an iced tea and they ordered the famous calamari as an appetizer.

"Did you ever get a chance to ask the computer guy about your emails?"

"Alec? I'll ask him tomorrow at school. Do you think the same guy who's sending the emails is the one who tried to set up the camera?"

"I don't know. It would be interesting to find out if the other murdered women were getting strange emails."

"Can you find out?" She tugged her sweater around her body.

"I intend to." He'd also intended this to be a relaxing dinner, not one loaded like a minefield with her mother's indiscretions and the threats against Michelle. Because he did see the emails and camera as threats.

He steered the conversation toward her teaching and discovered she'd spent a year in France. The rest of the meal passed quickly and Michelle's face lost its tightness, her body lost its rigidity.

He'd planned this dinner to soothe her and found that her company acted like a balm on him, as well. Her laugh gurgled and flowed over him, wearing down some of the rough edges he'd worn as a barrier since his escape from the Taliban.

A slow pulse beat in the base of his throat when he touched her hand. And he wasn't thinking about relaxing anymore.

The waiter placed a plate heaped with some kind of pie smothered in vanilla ice cream in the center of the table. "Compliments of the owner, Mr. Barbosa."

"I guess it pays to have friends in high places." Michelle dug her fork in the pie.

As Colin reached for his fork, his cell phone buzzed in his pocket. He rested the fork against the plate and pulled out the phone, showing it to Michelle. "It's Jake," he said, and answered.

"Jake, whaddya got?"

"Sorry I'm so late, man. I was working on a case, but it was no problem downloading this chip when I got back to the office."

"And?"

"Is the woman in question your girlfriend?"

Colin's gaze shifted to Michelle's huge brown eyes. "No."

"Friend?"

"Yeah. Get to it, Jake."

"Well, if she's your friend, you'd better keep an eye on her."

"Why is that?" Colin licked his lips, his eyes never leaving Michelle's.

"Because your lady friend has one serious stalker."

Chapter Nine

This can't be good. Colin looked ready to explode.

Michelle choked down her bite of apple pie, the sweet caramel turning to ash on her tongue. "What is it? What's he saying?"

Colin held up his index finger. "Uh-huh. Okay. Hold on a minute."

He swiveled the phone away from his mouth. "Michelle, what's your email address?"

She gave it to him and he repeated it into the phone.

"Thanks, Jake. I really appreciate it." He ended the call and tossed the phone onto the table.

"There was something on the camera?"

He walked his fingers across the table and entwined them with hers. "The chip was full. He's been watching you for a while."

Her fingers convulsed around his. "Y-you mean even before Amanda's murder?"

"It looks like it. The camera had a time stamp on it and a motion detector, so he wasn't wasting space on recording an empty room."

A chill rippled across her skin and she hunched her shoulders. "And my email address?"

"He's going to email the video to you, and I want to see what's on there."

"Uh, I'm not sure I do." Could he see her burning cheeks in the candlelight?

He pointed his fork at the pie, the ice cream dripping down the sides. "Do you want any more of that?"

"I lost my appetite."

"Always best to keep fortified when going into battle." He dug his fork into the pie and hacked off a huge bite.

"Is this a battle?" She wrinkled her nose, wondering how he was going to shovel that piece of pie into his mouth.

"It's gonna be."

Half an hour later, Colin pulled his car behind hers in the driveway. She exited the car on shaky legs. How bad could it be? A few nude shots of her floating from bedroom to bathroom? It's not like she'd been having wild orgies in her bedroom the past few weeks.

Once inside, Colin made a beeline for the laptop and flipped it open. "Do you need to log in?"

"I don't have a password. Just click on my email." She hovered behind him, clasping her purse to her chest.

Colin opened her in-box, and Jake's email was at the top of the list of new messages. His hand gripped the mouse. "Are you ready?"

"Do it. Whatever's on there isn't going to be a surprise to me."

He clicked on the message and then opened the attachment.

An image of her walking into the bedroom and tossing a sweatshirt onto the bed flickered across the computer monitor.

"Ah-ha, you're a secret slob."

She pinched his shoulder, grateful for his attempt to diffuse the tension that had her in an iron grip. "If you watch long enough, you'll see I put it away later."

The bathroom door closed and she came back into the

bedroom. She peeled off her T-shirt and dragged a blouse from a hanger in the closet. She walked out of the bedroom, stuffing her arms in the sleeves.

The screen turned gray, and a long sigh escaped from her lips. They continued to watch a few comings and goings. She entered the room again, toed off her shoes and began removing her clothes.

Her gaze darted to Colin's face, oddly illuminated by the glow from the laptop screen, almost satanic. She flicked a glance back to the screen where her other self was about to unhook her bra.

"I'll fast-forward through this. In fact, let me just get to the end to see if we can get an idea of how long he's been watching you."

Always the gentleman. But her stalker wasn't.

She had a stalker. Her blood pumped furiously through her veins. Her jaw tightened and her hands curled into fists. A noise must've escaped from her pursed lips because Colin twisted his head to the side.

"You okay?"

She ground her teeth before spitting out, "I'm pissed."

His eyes widened.

She spun away from him and the invasive images on the laptop and stalked to the front door. She whacked the palm of her hand against the wall. "How dare he? How dare he invade my privacy?"

Strong hands gripped her shoulders. "I'm glad the video got you hot. I was afraid you'd fall apart, but I should've known better."

Had the video gotten him hot, too?

She dragged her hands through her hair and turned to face him. His blue eyes darkened, and she hoped to God it wasn't with sympathy.

He curled a hand around her neck, pulling her into his

sphere. His lips brushed hers. Didn't feel sympathetic in the least.

Cupping the back of her head with his hand, he deepened the kiss and she tasted apple pie and cinnamon. She shifted her head to free her hair, and he broke away from her, leaving a cool emptiness.

"I'm sorry. That was dumb."

Was it? She touched her tingling lips with her fingertips.

"It's not because of that." He jerked a thumb over his shoulder. "It's not because I saw you on the video."

She placed a hand on his chest, the warmth of his skin beneath his shirt seeping into her palm. "I know that. I didn't figure a shot of me in my bra and panties would turn you into a sex-crazed maniac."

"Is that how I came across?" The corner of his mouth twitched. "A sex-crazed maniac?"

"Not at all." Laughing, she swiped the back of her hand across her forehead. The moment had floated out of their grasp, the video between them. "Look, are we going to turn the camera over to the police now that you've done all their work for them?"

"That's up to you. The camera doesn't have a serial number, so it's untraceable that way. I'm pretty sure no store in Coral Cove carries a spy camera like this. Most likely it was ordered off the internet with hundreds of places to choose from."

"So we're not going to find the owner and neither are the police?"

"I doubt it."

She brushed past him and sank to the couch. "Who is doing this and why? It must be the killer, Colin. It's the only thing that makes sense—too many coincidences otherwise. He probably spied on Amanda, too, before…"

"Maybe if we bring the camera to the police, they'll realize Chris Jeffers can't possibly be Amanda's killer. Then they'll get off their backsides and start doing some real police work."

She tilted her head against the cushion and stared at the ceiling. "Okay. Let's do it. Can you pick up the camera from Jake?"

"I'm doing that tomorrow morning."

"And can you bring it to the CCPD?" She slid her arm from the back of the couch and checked her watch. "I have school tomorrow."

"Then let's wrap this up." He strode to the laptop and closed out the video. "When Jake did the download, he didn't erase the video from the camera."

She pushed off the couch and stretched. "It's going to be a rough day tomorrow. I'm going to have a lot of curious kids in my classes."

"Maybe you should take the day off."

"It's the last week of school, and I have one more quiz to give them. Besides, I'm not running and hiding. Never did do that and I'm not about to start now."

"You did once."

She froze in midyawn and snapped her mouth shut. "What are you talking about?"

"That day on the beach. Do you remember? I found you down at the cove, in that semicircle of rocks."

Her heart did a flip in her chest. He remembered that? She'd sought refuge on the beach after some particularly vicious teasing about Mom and Eric. The gossip had reached a fever pitch that day, and she just hadn't been able to ignore it.

She tilted her head, ready to spew some lie about not exactly recalling the incident, but the serious expression in Colin's eyes had her swallowing the words. He'd brought it up for a reason, and it had more to do with him than her.

Dipping her chin, she said, "I do remember. I was crying about my mom and the whole sorry situation."

"And I left you there."

"I told you to leave."

"I should've stayed."

"I wanted to be alone, Colin, alone with my misery and embarrassment." She edged into the kitchen to get some water and to escape the intensity of his gaze.

"Maybe talking would've helped some of that misery and embarrassment."

She handed him a glass of water. "A teenage girl does not want to have a runny, red nose and puffy eyes when she's talking to the school jock."

His mouth stretched into a smile. "You looked great to me. Still do."

She took a sip of water, not knowing how to respond to his lie. She did *not* look great in high school, and at that particular moment in high school she'd probably looked even worse.

"It's getting late."

"Are you kicking me out?"

"I do have to make it to work on time tomorrow. Thanks for a great dinner and thanks for getting the video on the camera uploaded, even though it's not exactly what I wanted to see."

"You're welcome, but I'm not going anywhere."

She jerked her hand and the water sloshed over the rim. "You're not?"

"There's a killer out there, Michelle. And you may be next on his list."

"Thanks for reminding me."

"You need reminding, and you need to stay mad. He took your friend, he stole your privacy."

"And you're going to camp out on my couch to make sure he doesn't make a return visit?"

"Damn straight."

Her blood sang in her veins and a thrill zigzagged up her back. He wanted to be here. He wanted to protect her. And maybe some of that had to do with his guilt over leaving his brother behind in Afghanistan, but right now she'd take it.

She shrugged. "It's your back. Do you at least want a sleeping bag so you can stretch out on the floor?"

"Sure. I might be here for a while."

Michelle ducked into the spare bedroom she used as an office and dragged the sleeping bag from the closet. She stopped at her bedroom door, hugging the sleeping bag to her chest and staring at the bedroom window.

Bring it on, pervert. I have my own personal bodyguard now.

COLIN LISTENED TO THE shower and fantasized about its inhabitant. In the video, Michelle's body, clad only in lacy underwear, had been long and lithe, her movements graceful and sensuous.

He punched his pillow. He was as bad as the perv who'd placed the camera.

He unzipped the sleeping bag and peeled it open. He should get out of here and let Michelle get started with her day. He'd pick up the spy cam from Jake and drop in on the Coral Cove P.D. and see what he could do to convince them they'd arrested the wrong man.

By the time Michelle bustled into the kitchen, fresh from her shower and dressed in a skirt and light sweater, he had the teakettle bubbling and a bagel in the toaster oven.

Her eyebrows shot up. "Bodyguard *and* cook?"

He dipped his head into the fridge for the tub of cream cheese to cool his flushed face. God, he hoped she hadn't pegged him as some perfect human specimen. He'd had enough of that…and it was a far cry from the truth.

He dropped the container on the counter. "A toasted bagel and boiling water does not a cook make. Just paying you back for yesterday."

She slid past him into the kitchen, her hair tickling his bare chest, and he inhaled her fresh scent—lemon shampoo and a dab of some flowery perfume. He could've lived on that smell alone in captivity.

"Thanks. It's perfect."

Uh-oh. There goes that word again. "It's the least I can do for keeping you up past your bedtime last night, and now I'm going to get out of your way so you can finish getting ready for school."

"Keep me posted if anything comes up." She plucked the hot bagel from the toaster oven with her fingertips and dropped it onto a plate. "School is out at two forty-five, but I'll be there late for the robotics club party. I'm the adviser."

He grinned. "You really are a math geek, aren't you?"

"Yep." She licked a line of cream cheese from the knife.

His jeans got uncomfortably tight. Who knew geeks could be so damned sexy?

Colin backed out of the kitchen and swept his shirt from the back of the couch. "Have a good day, and be careful out there."

He drove the hundred yards back up the street to his folks' place, slowing to a crawl as he cruised past Columbella House. The house had never haunted his dreams, but after poking around the basement the other day he had to admit Columbella gave off a weird vibe.

Unexplained disappearances, a murder and a few suicides would do that to a house.

When he got to his parents' place, he showered and changed. On the way out of town he hit the fast-food drive-through for a breakfast burrito and a cup of joe. Michelle's coffee tasted much better.

Michelle tasted much better.

He'd been a total idiot kissing her right after he'd watched her undressing on the computer screen. The video hadn't turned him on at all. It had sickened him. Made him burn with red-hot rage.

What kind of coward watched a woman without her permission? A killer.

The burrito he'd just inhaled sat like a rock in his stomach. He'd bet his '65 T-Bird sitting in his garage in L.A. that this guy had been watching Tiffany, Belinda and Amanda, too. Of the three murdered women only Tiffany had been married. Belinda had been single and Amanda separated. And they'd all graduated together. That had to be the key, but the Coral Cove cops and that mayor had placed all their hopes on Chris.

It shouldn't be too hard to figure out who in this town had traveled to San Francisco and Vegas. Of course, maybe the killer didn't even live here and happened to be in town for the reunion.

So many scenarios. Too many to feel comfortable leaving Michelle on her own at night. He had to stay there for her protection.

He snorted to himself. *Yeah, like that's the only reason you want to camp out in her living room.*

He drove another forty miles with the ocean out his right-hand window until he pulled off the highway and made his way to the sheriff's station. Jake had already told him he was on duty.

Colin breezed through the glass doors of the sheriff's station, flashed his FBI badge and asked for Jake. He wended his way through the desks in the back of the room and poked his head into a small, bare office where Jake was parked in front of a computer.

"Do they keep you chained to that thing, or what?"

Jake glanced up and then pushed away from the desk. He strode forward with his hand outstretched. "Don't see you for years and then you show your mug twice in two days."

He pumped Jake's hand. "Thanks for uploading the video from that camera so quickly and getting back to me."

"No problem." He kicked out a chair for Colin. "Like you said, they keep me chained to my computer, anyway."

Colin spun the chair around and straddled it. "Any news about the guy CCPD has in custody for the Amanda murder?"

"Still waiting for the labs to come back on the blood smear. If it belongs to the victim, they're going to charge him."

"Maybe not, when I drop off the camera used to spy on Michelle."

"If they find a similar camera at the victim's house, they might listen to you. Otherwise, Chief Evans will dismiss this baby—" he held up the spy camera "—as a one-off crime—a peeping Tom checking in on your friend."

"I've gotta get through to them somehow. The killer is still out there, and he has Michelle pegged as his next victim."

"Chief Evans knows you're not officially on the cases of the other women, right?"

"Yep."

Jake shook his head. "He's not gonna give you squat, dude."

"Then I guess I'll just have to take it." He held out his hand for the camera, and Jake dropped it into his palm. "I'm going to head back now and see if I can change his mind."

"This woman, Michelle, a special friend of yours?"

She hadn't been before he'd made the trip up here—just another graduate of a class some killer seemed to be targeting. But she'd become more than a potential victim, more than a woman in need of protection. More.

"Yeah, she's special."

Jake tapped his cheekbone beneath his eye. "You'd better keep a close watch on her, because this killer is one sick puppy."

MICHELLE GRIPPED THE KNIFE and waved it in the air. "Anyone want more cake?"

A handful of teenage boys clambered over desks and each other to the front of the classroom. Where did they put all the food they consumed?

She sliced another row of pieces from the chocolate cake and flipped them onto paper plates. She stuck plastic forks into the cake, and the boys snapped up the offerings.

Speaking above the chatter, Michelle said, "Don't even think about leaving this classroom until you've picked up your trash."

The kids who weren't shoveling cake into their mouths gathered up the cups, plates and almost-empty bags of chips and tossed them into the large plastic garbage bag Michelle had brought in for the occasion. They were a good group of kids, enjoyed math and problem solving. Geeks, as Colin had dubbed them. And she still fit right in.

"Do you need help inputting today's quiz grades in the computer, Ms. Girard?" Eden, Michelle's teacher's assistant, perched on the edge of her desk, swinging her leg.

"That's okay. You can take off…after this mess is cleaned up."

"Thanks, Ms. Girard." The girl's gaze slid to one of the boys now licking frosting off a paper plate.

Michelle bit her lip to hide her smile—amazing what

teenage girls found attractive in the opposite sex. Her own high school crush had been perfect…still was.

She pulled her cell phone out of her pocket to check the time and for any messages. Colin told her he'd leave her a message if anything important happened. He had to be back from the sheriff's station by now. He'd probably even dropped off the camera at the CCPD. Would it make Chief Evans reevaluate his suspect?

"Ms. Girard, can I take home the chips?" One of the boys held up three bags.

"Just one bag. See if anyone else wants the rest. And if anyone wants a piece of cake to go, help yourselves, but if I see any cake in the hallway or on school grounds, I'll hunt you down."

The students finished cleaning the room and claiming the rest of the leftover food. They thanked her for supervising the club and all promised to be back the next school year.

Michelle centered her keyboard on the desk and slumped in her chair. Three more days of school and two more days of quizzes to give, grade and enter in the computer. The computer program they used calculated the percentages automatically and compiled the final course grade. Made life a lot simpler.

She powered on the computer and navigated to the grading program with a few clicks. She ducked to retrieve the quizzes from her bottom drawer, popping up when she heard the chime from her computer indicating new email.

She hoped it wasn't from some parent who'd just realized his precious child was going to fail algebra. Holding her breath, she displayed her in-box.

A message from Sue Daniels, the geometry teacher, popped up and Michelle opened it. Crud, Sue needed Scantrons for her final exam tomorrow and didn't have her key to the supply cabinet. She'd left for the day, didn't want to interrupt the robotics party and wanted Michelle to slip thirty Scantrons under her classroom door.

Sue was notoriously late, always rushing to class at the last minute. She didn't exactly admit that she wouldn't get to school early enough tomorrow to get her own Scantrons, but Michelle understood the plea.

She dipped again to her bottom drawer for some Scantrons for Sue, but one lonely Scantron nestled in the file folder.

Sighing, Michelle pushed back from her desk and snagged her keys from her purse. She locked her desk and then locked her classroom behind her. She didn't want any kids sneaking in there and changing grades.

She started down the empty hallway, her heels clicking on the polished linoleum. Tony, the custodian, must've already cleaned this floor.

Her fingers floating above the handrail, Michelle trotted down the steps to the first floor. The silence of the school closed in on her. Bereft of students and clanging locker doors and the incessant bells, the halls seemed almost unwelcoming, as if she'd intruded on their private time.

She turned the corner to the faculty lounge and the supply closet next to it and tripped to a stop. The supply closet door was open a sliver.

The teachers could get into big trouble for leaving the closet unlocked or open. Greg Ochoa, the principal, guarded the room like Fort Knox. As long as nothing important was missing, Michelle had no intention of ratting out any of her colleagues.

She approached the closet and faltered. A tingling sensation swept up her back and settled at the base of her neck. Gripping the doorjamb, she glanced over her left shoulder at the empty corridor.

"Tony?"

Her voice echoed. He must be in one of the other buildings by now.

She bumped the open door with her hip. A heavy, metallic odor flooded her senses. Her gaze dropped. A rivulet of thick blood meandered toward the toe of her shoe.

And the high school counselor's mouth gaped open in a silent scream.

Chapter Ten

Michelle covered her hands with her mouth and gagged. She backpedaled and banged her elbow on the doorjamb. The jolt lit a fire under her feet and she scrambled backward, slipping on the polished floor.

She crashed to the linoleum, the side of her hip hitting the floor with a smack. Her stare still pinned to the dead body in the closet, she twisted onto her backside and struggled to her feet.

Her head whipped from left to right. She screamed. "Tony!"

She moved at a fast limp toward the staircase. She could go up to her room, lock herself inside and call 9-1-1 from there. But would the killer allow her to make it to her room and the cell phone sitting on her desk?

Her gaze darted toward the door leading to the quad. Would there be students out there? Teachers in their rooms?

The maniac who had just slit Jenny Procter's throat?

Her grasp on the handrail of the staircase tightened, her knuckles whitening. She tracked up the stairs with her eyes. Or was he waiting for her by her classroom? In her classroom?

She spun around and rushed for the double doors. Slamming down on the release bar she shoved at the door. It banged into a body and she screamed.

She turned and hobbled toward the stairs. A voice stopped her in her tracks.

"Michelle?"

The low voice engulfed her in warm relief and she sobbed as she staggered toward the safety of Colin's arms.

He scooped her close to his chest and smoothed his hands down her back, ironing out the chills that racked her body. "My God, what's wrong?"

She gulped air into her lungs, but her tongue wouldn't move to form any words. She thrust an arm behind her, pointing a shaky finger down the hall.

"There's something in one of the classrooms?"

"A-around the corner in the supply closet. A body."

The muscles in Colin's body hardened, as if he'd turned to stone. He cinched an arm around her waist and took two steps.

"What's wrong with your leg?"

"I fell. I hurt my hip."

"I'm not leaving you here." He swept her up in his arms as if she were five feet tall instead of five feet ten inches tall. "Get my phone out of my shirt pocket and call 9-1-1."

She slid the cell out of his pocket and made the call while he continued to stride down the hall. She tapped his shoulder. "To the right. The last door on the right."

He turned the corner and she slid down his body to her feet. Removing his gun, he held his hand up. "Wait here."

She leaned against the wall, her hands flat behind her. The police would be here any minute. Colin had his gun out. Nothing to worry about.

Except the dead body in the closet.

She held her breath as Colin nudged the door wide with his arm. It must've swung back when she'd hightailed it out of there.

He cursed. "Who is she?"

"She's Jenny Procter, the high school guidance counselor."

Leaning forward into the closet, he said, "Her throat's slit."

"I—I saw that. So much blood."

Sirens wailed again, just like at Columbella House. Only this time, the CCPD wouldn't be as happy with their discovery—another dead body, not a convenient suspect just in time for the summer rush.

Colin backed out of the closet. "Did you see anything? Anybody?"

Michelle shook her head.

"How did you happen to find her?"

"I came down here to get Scantrons for myself and another teacher."

"That's a coincidence." Colin dug a hand through his dark hair, a crease forming between his eyebrows.

The sirens had come to a halt in front of the school. Michelle had reported the building and the room number, and soon law enforcement would be swarming the school.

She limped toward Colin and gripped his arm. "Colin?"

He looked down into her eyes, the furrow on his brow deepening. "Yeah?"

"Jenny Procter graduated from Coral Cove High School ten years ago."

COLIN SLID HIS WEAPON into his gun bag as he heard the CCPD burst through the double doors. He squeezed Michelle's cold hand and poked his head around the corner. "We're down here."

The officers moved swiftly on their rubber-soled shoes, their duty belts squeaking and clinking with each step. Chief Evans brought up the rear, a scowl darkening his face.

"What the hell happened? Is this some kind of joke, Michelle?"

"Joke?" Michelle's mouth fell open. "Jenny Procter is in that closet with her throat slit, and I found her. The only joke is that guy you have sitting in your jail, Chief."

Colin tugged on Michelle's hand. She could whip up her anger in a second…and he liked it. She'd grown out of her shyness with both barrels blazing.

Chief Evans swore and smacked his fist against the wall. "What does it look like in there, Norris?"

The young uniform from Amanda's murder withdrew from the closet, a little green around the gills. "It's Jenny Procter, sir, and she's dead. Throat slit, just like Sarge's wife."

"And why are all these women dying on your doorstep?" The chief narrowed his eyes at Michelle as if he blamed her.

Colin shifted his weight to his left foot, blocking Michelle from Evans's inspection. "I tried to explain that when I dropped off the spy camera, Chief. We have a serial killer who's targeting the women of a particular Coral Cove graduating class, the one that's having its ten-year reunion in a few weeks, Michelle's class."

The chief growled and stalked toward the closet, shooing his officers out of the way.

Michelle rested her forehead on Colin's shoulder. "He has some nerve, doesn't he? He's just ticked off that this is happening on his watch before he takes his next job."

"Are you okay?" He swept a lock of hair from her smooth cheek. "I want to take you home. Do you need to see a doctor about your hip?"

She sighed, her soft breath warming the skin through his T-shirt. "I just bruised it."

"Then you need some ice and some ibuprofen, not Chief Evans's hostile questions."

While the chief got more information from Michelle, the officers rounded up the school custodian and two teachers who'd been in another building for questioning.

One of the teachers had seen the victim walking across the quad at about four o'clock and figured she'd been heading for the teacher's lounge, where several school staff members left their lunches in the fridge.

The county coroner arrived, along with the CSI team and Lieutenant Trammell, who'd been handling Amanda's case. Law-enforcement personnel jammed the corridor and curious onlookers had begun to gather in the quad.

"Can we leave, Chief?" Michelle looked about ready to collapse. She needed to get off her feet, and Colin would carry her out of here if he had to.

"Yeah, yeah." He waved his hands. "But stick around. You two are involved in this up to your eyeballs."

Michelle touched Colin's arm. "I need to go to my classroom to get my purse and bag."

They got by the officer stationed at the staircase, and Michelle leaned on Colin for support to make it up the stairs.

Colin had his own questions for Michelle, but he'd wait until he got her home and comfortable.

She unlocked her classroom door and limped toward her desk. She stuffed some file folders in her bag, and then braced her hands on the desk, hunching over. "How are we going to finish out the school year this week? How can the seniors celebrate their graduation with Ms. Procter dead, murdered on school grounds?"

Colin came up behind her and put his arms around her waist. "Don't think about that right now. It's not your decision to make. Was she married? Kids?"

"Divorced. That's why she came back to her hometown. She'd met a guy at the University of Washington, where she'd gone to school. She stayed up there after the marriage and when it ended, she returned to Coral Cove." A single tear dripped onto the desk blotter.

"Let's get you home."

Colin rode the tail of Michelle's bumper like he expected the bogeyman to jump out and snatch her from her car. How the hell had she just happened to wind up at that supply closet at the same time as a dead body?

And if the killer lured her there, why hadn't he finished her off when he had the chance? Maybe something scared him away. Maybe he saw the custodian or one of the other teachers.

Colin pulled his car in behind Michelle's. The CCPD had removed the crime scene tape from Amanda's murder site. Take down one crime scene, put up another. They could've reused the tape.

When they walked through the front door, Colin leveled a finger at the couch. "Sit."

Michelle's lips twisted as she lowered herself to the couch.

Colin headed for the kitchen, calling over his shoulder. "Do you have any ice packs?"

"I'm a runner. I have ice packs in the freezer."

"Did you run track in high school?" He yanked open the freezer door and snatched an ice pack from the second shelf. He wrapped it in a paper towel and filled the teakettle with water. Tea always helped in these situations, didn't it?

He carried the cold pack to the living room between his fingers and kneeled beside the couch where Michelle had tilted her head back on a cushion, her eyes closed. "Well, did you?"

She opened one eye. "Did I what?"

"Run track in high school?"

"I didn't do anything in high school except study and a few clubs."

He held out the pack. "Where does it hurt?"

She pressed her fingertips against the side of her hip and drew in a sharp gasp. "Right about there."

Colin gingerly placed the ice pack on the soft material of her skirt, where it clung to the curve of her hip. He patted it. "Hold that there."

Her fingers brushed his as she pressed the pack against her hip. Her touch ignited a slow burn in his belly. He'd never wanted a woman more, and the timing had never been worse.

The teakettle whistled and he rose to his feet. The last thing Michelle needed was a seduction.

She blinked long lashes over her brown eyes, like two pools of melted chocolate. "Tea, too? You've turned into a regular Florence Nightingale."

"Maybe I have ulterior motives." He turned his back on her to let her mull that over.

He poured the boiling water over a tea bag and dunked the bag a few times. "Ibuprofen?"

"I have some in my purse."

He carried the steaming tea in front of him and placed it on the coffee table within her reach. "Does Han Ting still deliver or do you want pizza?"

"Dinner, too?" She leaned forward, picked up the mug and cradled it between her hands.

"It's almost six o'clock. I don't know about you, but I'm starving."

Michelle pulled her cell phone along with a small pill bottle from her purse and tossed him the phone. "I have the number in my contacts. Just order something spicy."

He placed the order and dropped the phone on the couch next to her. He reached across her lap. "Keep this ice on your hip."

She blew on her tea and gave him a measured look over the rim of the cup. "Stop stalling, Roarke. I know you're antsy to get to the bottom of this latest murder."

He exhaled a long, slow breath. He should've figured Michelle wouldn't play the victim for long. "I know you stayed late for the party, but why didn't you leave right after?"

"I wanted to input the quiz grades in our grading program. I'm sure that's why those other teachers were still there, too."

"What brought you down to the supply closet at that particular moment? I know you said you needed Scantrons, but why then?" He held his breath. Her answer was crucial to understanding how the killer had lured her downstairs.

"I got an email from another math teacher. She had already left. She had an early-morning final exam, forgot to stock some Scantrons in her classroom and asked me to slip a batch under her door."

"You didn't have any in your desk?"

"I thought I did but I didn't have any, either, so that's when I went down to the supply closet...and found Jenny."

The ice pack had slid between the cushions, and Colin scooped it out and pressed it against Michelle's hip. He left his hand there, his arm across her lap. "Do you know for sure that this math teacher sent the email?"

She slurped her tea and choked on it. "It came from her school email address. We all have the same address with our first initial and last name at the beginning."

"I thought she was at home?"

"We can bring our laptops home, and we have remote access to the school network. So we can be logged in to the school system and use the school's email."

He plucked up the cell phone again. "Do me a favor and call her. Ask her if she sent that email."

There was a slight tremble to Michelle's hand when she took the phone from his. She punched a few buttons and waited. "Hi, Sue. I suppose you heard the news about Jenny Procter. I'm wondering if we're going to finish out the school year. Anyway, I was wondering about that email you sent me about the Scantrons. Can you give me a call back on my cell?" She hung up.

"You think the killer sent me that email to lure me downstairs, don't you?"

"Yeah, I do, Michelle. It's all too coincidental otherwise."

She dropped her gaze to the pale green liquid in her cup. "Do you think he planned to kill me, too?"

"Probably." He placed his cold hand against her warm thigh. "I'm sorry, but I think so."

Her fingers tightened on the handle of her cup. "Don't be sorry for telling me what you think, Colin. I need to hear it. What did the police say about the camera on my window?"

He snorted. "Not much, since they still believed they had their guy locked up right and tight. They figured Coral Cove had a Peeping Tom."

"Instead of a serial killer."

"They need to start warning the women of Coral Cove, especially the ones in your graduating class." He traced the ridges of her knuckles. "You want the truth, Michelle? I left something out at the school."

He could see the pulse beating in her throat and inexplicably he wanted to lay his lips against the spot.

"Yes?"

"There were rose petals in that closet."

The cup jerked in her hand and the tea scurried up the sides and sloshed back down again. "Of course there were."

They both jumped when the doorbell rang.

He squeezed her knee. "That's our kung pao chicken."

Colin tucked his Glock in the back of his waistband, anyway, and opened the door slowly. The computer whiz stood on the front porch and adjusted his glasses as if he couldn't believe his eyes.

Colin pointed to Alec's hard-sided briefcase. "I suppose you don't have any kung pao chicken in there."

"N-no." He peered around Colin's shoulder. "Is Michelle home?"

"Is that Alec?"

Colin stepped aside. There went his cozy dinner with Michelle…discussing a murder. "C'mon in, man. You heard the news about the school counselor?"

"Of course. It's all over town." Alec swung his briefcase to his chest and hugged it, the veins in his corded arms popping.

Michelle slid her legs from the coffee table. "It's horrible, Alec."

"Stay where you are, and get that ice pack back on your hip." Colin stalked toward the couch. "In fact, I'm going to get you a colder one."

Michelle resumed her previous position and rolled her eyes. "Have a seat, Alec. Have you heard anything about the rest of the school year?"

"We're taking a break tomorrow, but resuming the next day which will be the last day of school. Graduation will take place on Friday instead of Thursday."

Colin returned with a fresh ice pack and replaced the other one. He kept his hand on Michelle's hip to gauge Alec's reaction.

Alec dropped his gaze to Colin's hand, and the color in his face heightened.

"How did you find out all that? Greg didn't call me."

"Probably didn't want to disturb you. We all heard you were the one who found Jenny."

"So you came over here to tell me the new schedule?"

He tilted his chin. "And to check out your laptop. You asked me if I could take a look and see if I could retrieve those deleted emails. It might be more important than ever."

"It was an email address from one of those free email services if that helps."

"Do you mind?" Alec half rose from his chair, holding himself up with his hands gripping the arms of the chair.

The veins in his sinewy forearms popped and Colin noted that for a skinny guy, Alec had a lot of strength.

Michelle wiggled her fingers in the direction of her laptop on the kitchen table. "Help yourself. There's no password."

"Maybe you should set one." Alec pulled out the chair and settled into it as if he had every intention of parking himself there for hours.

The doorbell rang again and Michelle clapped her hands together. "That has to be the Chinese food."

Colin paid the delivery guy and carried the bag into the kitchen. "Alec, you want some food?"

Alec looked up from his key-tapping. "That's okay. I'm going to get something later."

Right answer. Colin dipped into the cartons and filled up two plates. He carried them to the couch and handed one to Michelle. "How's the hip?"

She poked it with her index finger. "Frozen."

Colin tried to settle on superficial topics and every time Michelle tried to steer him back to the murders, he found another inane issue to discuss. He didn't trust Alec. He didn't trust anyone right now. How did Michelle know Alec wasn't deleting every last email in her in-box?

Alec jumped up from the table, rubbing his hands together. "Okay. That's it."

"You retrieved them already?" Michelle shifted on the couch, rolling onto her uninjured hip.

"Not quite. I'm running a deleted mail recovery utility. It has to do its scan, but it'll rescue all deleted emails from the past few months and put them in another folder where you can view them and then save them. Save the ones you need and I'll be back to see if I can trace the IP address."

"Thanks, Alec."

"No problem. Take care of yourself." He slipped out the front door, lugging his briefcase along with him.

"That was fast." Colin sauntered to the computer to watch green numbers scrolling across a black screen. "He didn't say how long it would take."

"As long as it takes." She held up her chopsticks. "Do you want the last piece of shrimp?"

Colin dropped onto the cushion next to her and plucked the shrimp from her chopsticks with his teeth.

Color ebbed into her cheeks and she dropped the chopsticks onto her plate with a clatter. "Are you going to tell me why you didn't want to discuss the murders in front of Alec?"

"Do you trust him?"

"Alec?" Her eyes widened. "You don't suspect Alec?"

"Anyone in this town is a possible suspect." He shoved the plates back and propped his shoe on the table. "You do realize the killer is someone who lives here in Coral Cove?"

She twisted her fingers into knots. "Not necessarily. It could be someone from a neighboring city. It could be a visitor."

"For a visitor, he sure knows his way around town. And then there's the connection between the victims—all Coral Cove High graduates from the same class."

"You saw the petals in the supply closet."

"Pink."

"Did Detective Marsh believe you this time?"

"The crime scene team bagged them, and I still have the petals from Amanda's murder scene."

"Do you think the cops are going to take another look at the video from that spy camera?" Her cheeks turned as pink as those rose petals. "I—I mean, do you think they'll take the video more seriously now?"

"I think they will. If they have any sense, they'll go through your graduating class and make a note of all the girls. For all we know, there could've been more murders in other states that nobody thought to tie to the murders of Belinda Frank and Tiffany Gunderson."

He stacked the plates and carried them to the sink. "In fact, we should do that ourselves. Do you have your yearbook handy?"

Michelle's cell phone played its song and she grabbed it. "Hi, Sue."

Colin paused to watch the laptop go through its paces, keeping his head cocked toward Michelle's conversation.

"I know it's terrible. I can't believe it."

She clutched the small phone with two hands, pressing it against her ear. "The Scantrons. You sent an email asking me to get some for you from the supply closet."

Michelle sucked in a sharp breath and slumped against the back of the couch.

Guess Sue didn't send that email, after all.

"SCANTRONS? I NEVER SENT YOU an email, Michelle. Larry dropped off a huge stack for me last week so I wouldn't run out during finals."

The blood was thundering in Michelle's ears and she felt almost too weak to hold the phone. She forced the words past her tight throat, aware that Colin had parked himself in front of her. "I must've misread the email."

"Maybe it was from Daniel Sharp, and you just figured it was from me because I'm such an airhead. Anyway, I don't think anyone's going to be getting Scantrons out of that closet for a while."

Michelle ended the call and dropped the phone in her lap. "You were right to be suspicious. Sue didn't send the email."

"Do you think you really misread the email address?" Colin perched on the coffee table across from her.

"No. The email was from Sue Daniels's email address and someone even put her name at the end of the message."

"Then someone has access to her computer."

"Or someone hacked her computer and was able to send out a message that looked like it was from her address."

"You know what this means?" He lifted her feet and shifted them to his lap.

As he kneaded her instep, Michelle closed her eyes. She just wanted to float away. She didn't want to think about any of this anymore. She wanted to meet Colin again in some peaceful place.

Of course, in some peaceful place Colin wouldn't be sitting here rubbing her feet. He couldn't resist a poor damsel needing a good rescue.

She slipped her feet from his lap and braced them against the edge of the table. "It means Jenny's killer lured me down to the supply closet to make me victim number five."

Colin's blue eyes hardened to chips of ice. "I'm not going to let that happen. I'm not going to leave you until the cops catch this guy."

"Do you think they will?" And when they did, how fast would Colin hightail it out of Coral Cove?

"He's brash. He murdered in broad daylight at a school. He's going to make a mistake. He already made a mistake." Holding out his hand, Colin said, "Give me your phone. I'm going to call them right now and tell them about the fake email."

Michelle dropped her phone into Colin's palm and struggled to her feet. She held up her hand when he began to protest. "I need to stretch. The ibuprofen and ice really helped."

He sat back down and made his call to the police while Michelle shuffled into the kitchen and got two sodas from the fridge. She paused at her laptop, humming away. Whoever was sending these threats had to be computer literate, but she refused to consider Alec. She couldn't consider anyone she knew. But the killer had to be someone with a connection to her graduating class.

Colin ended the call and Michelle handed him a soda. "Sorry, no beer."

"Yeah, yeah, I know. You don't drink. Any particular reason why not?"

"My mom did." She shrugged and took a swig of her soda. "What did the cops have to say?"

"Sue's classroom was one of several rooms, including the supply closet, that someone broke into. Anyone could've accessed her computer and email."

"None of this would've happened at the school if we'd had those cameras." She twisted the tab off her can. "We were going to install cameras on campus, but we didn't have the money."

"A local would know all about the lack of cameras."

She glanced at the whirring laptop and sighed.

Colin rose from the coffee table and then stepped over it in one long stride. He pulled her close, resting his hands lightly on her hips. "You've had enough for the day. Is your hip still sore?"

She shook her head and he swept her hair back with one hand, cupping the back of her head. The slight pressure he exerted tilted her head back until she was staring into his eyes.

His gaze dropped to her lips and she moistened them with her tongue in a gesture of nervousness. He misread the gesture.

He dipped his head and sealed his mouth over hers. The

fire in his kiss drained her of any shred of resistance she'd been considering.

She curled her arms around his neck and kissed him back. She was grateful for his protection. Grateful for his help. But the way she moved her lips against his didn't have one ounce of gratefulness in it.

She wanted him.

His hands slid from her hips to her backside. He pressed her closer still until she could feel his desire for her, hot and hard.

He wanted her, too.

The room heated up, making a mockery of the wisps of damp fog that swirled around the house. She massaged circles down his back, committing every hard muscle and flat plane to memory. Her hands tingled with impatience to feel his bare skin slide beneath her touch.

His kisses trailed from her lips along her jaw. He nibbled her earlobe and she giggled. "Ticklish?"

"Are you?" She slipped her hands beneath his T-shirt and ran them up his sides.

He shivered and stepped back, whispering in her ear. "Take it off."

She grasped the edge of his shirt and yanked it up as he raised his arms above his head. The shirt got caught on his chin. He gave a muffled laugh and pulled it off.

Her greedy fingers trailed from his collarbone over the sculpted muscles of his chest down to his flat belly. Even across his stomach, hard ridges lined up in an even six-pack.

The flat red scars crisscrossing his chest couldn't even mar the beauty of his form. She traced the convoluted path of the scars with the tip of her finger.

He closed his eyes, his black lashes like spiky crescents. "Does it hurt?"

"Not at all. I've just never… Nobody has ever…"

Ducking her head she replaced her fingertips with her lips and laid a row of kisses along each scar. Colin trembled at her assault.

Then he plowed his fingers through her hair and lifted her head. He unbuttoned the small buttons on her sweater with deft hands until it gaped open, falling from her shoulders and revealing her lacy white bra.

Sliding a thumb beneath one bra strap, he tugged it off her shoulder. He nuzzled her neck as he cupped her breast with his hand. The pad of his thumb rasped across the silky material of her bra, circling her peaked nipple.

Her heart pounded beneath his touch and she threw her head back. He ran his tongue up the side of her exposed neck and slipped his fingers inside her bra.

When his large, rough hand met the bare skin of her breast, Michelle moaned. She couldn't help it. The intensity of their connection had dragged the sound from her lips. She arched her back to fill his hand.

"You're so beautiful." He trailed his hand up her back with a featherlight touch. He tugged at the clasp of her bra until it unhooked, and then peeled the tangled mess of sweater and bra from her shoulders.

Goose bumps trickled across her body, and Colin clasped her against him. When bare skin met bare skin, Michelle's blood sizzled. She raked her nails across Colin's back and tucked her fingers in the waistband of his jeans.

She couldn't believe they were still standing, exploring each other, afraid to move from that spot as if any movement would break the spell of wonder they felt in each other's bodies. She inched her fingers along his waist until they stumbled across his fly. She yanked at the top button and then nearly screamed when she discovered the rest of the buttons instead of a zipper.

Some involuntary sound must've escaped her lips because

Colin chuckled and reached down to expertly unbutton his jeans. She pushed his hands away and peeled the jeans open, yanking them from his hips.

She tucked her hand inside his jeans, wondering boxers or briefs, and discovered…commando. A pulse beat low in her throat and she swallowed. She skimmed her palm against his hard smooth flesh.

She'd never wanted anything so much in her life as she wanted to feel him inside her—solid, strong, sweet.

A car alarm blared. Michelle jumped back, bumping Colin's chin.

"What?" She blinked her eyes. The harsh noise of the alarm punched holes in her pink, puffy dream cloud.

Colin stepped back from her with a shudder. He yanked up his jeans without buttoning them and stalked to the window. "It must be your car. I don't think my rental has an alarm."

Michelle swept her sweater from the floor and clutching it to her chest, reached for her purse. She hooked a finger around her key chain and yanked her keys from the purse's front pocket. She jabbed at the alarm button on the remote and the alarm stopped blasting.

Colin turned from the window and met her eyes. "I'm going to have a look."

Her sore hip throbbed and she stuffed her arms into the sleeves of her sweater. "I'm coming with you."

Colin buttoned his jeans and unzipped the gun bag he'd tossed on the kitchen counter hours ago. He gripped the weapon in his right hand and prowled toward the front door.

Michelle followed him into the fog that danced around them. It plucked at her hair with damp fingers, settling against her warm skin with prickles of moisture. The marine layer had crept up on them while they'd been snug in the house, oblivious to the encroaching white haze that had wiped out all visibility more than one foot in front of them.

Her car squatted in the driveway, a dark shape holding secrets. Colin aimed the flashlight on it, illuminating the side.

"No broken windows on this side." He flipped the door handle. "Still locked."

"Maybe we had a little earthquake, which jostled it." Michelle hunched her shoulders and rubbed her arms.

He turned and smiled, his white teeth gleaming in the mist. "If there had been a seven point oh, I'm sure I wouldn't have noticed."

She grinned, grateful he couldn't see her warm, schoolgirl cheeks. Grateful he'd broken the eerie spell of the fog that had wrapped them in cotton.

Colin circled the car, the beam from his flashlight playing over the bumper and trunk. Reaching out, Michelle grabbed the belt loop of his pants. She didn't want to be left behind.

When he sidled around the left front bumper, he froze and Michelle bumped into his bare back, which had stiffened.

"What's wrong?" She peered around his broad frame and choked.

One word had been scrawled across her windshield: *Slut*.

Chapter Eleven

Scorching fury beat against Colin's temples. He wanted to smash something. He wanted to smash the windshield that harbored the hurtful word...the threatening word.

Michelle trembled beside him. He clamped a hand on her shoulder and spun her around. "Let's get back inside and call the cops."

"He was here, wasn't he?" She cranked her head from side to side. "He was out here while we..."

He marched her up the steps and slammed the door behind them. *Dammit.* The guy had been right under his nose and Colin had been busy lusting after Michelle when he should've been protecting her. He'd been too concerned with his own desires to keep her safe.

Looking out for number one...again.

When he called the CCPD, he got Officer Donnelly on the phone and told him about the message on Michelle's car. "I understand you have a murder to investigate...two murders, but the vandalism to Michelle's car is linked to those murders."

Michelle whispered. "Are they going to come out?"

"Yeah. We'll leave it." He shook his head at Michelle. "You checked out Sue's computer?"

Officer Donnelly told him Sue Daniels's computer had been vandalized and there was no way to verify whether or not the email sent to Michelle had come from Sue's school laptop.

Donnelly also told him they'd released Chris Jeffers from jail.

Colin asked Donnelly to keep him informed and ended the call. He squeezed his eyes shut and pinched the bridge of his nose. "Did you get that?"

"Something about Sue's laptop being damaged…and nobody is coming to check out my car."

"Sit." He patted the sofa cushion beside him. "They're going to send someone out tomorrow."

She perched stiffly beside him on the couch, her hands on her knees primly pressed together. "And Sue's computer?"

"Someone physically damaged it. Did you hear anything from your classroom?"

"No, but her room is down the hall from mine on the other side of the staircase." She wedged her hands between her knees. "Colin, if the killer was already on school property, in my building, down the hall mucking with Sue's email and computer, why didn't he just come to my room and… you know, finish me off?"

He rasped his knuckles against his stubble. "If he had come charging into your classroom, he would've lost the element of surprise. You would've put up a fight, made some noise. He couldn't afford that."

"So you think he lured Jenny to the supply close and surprised her?"

"Most likely. The cops are checking Jenny's emails, too."

"Then something or someone must've scared him off when I went down there."

"The custodian? Another teacher?" He rubbed her ramrod straight back. "Who knows? Maybe he didn't want to push his luck twice in one day."

"But he came over to warn me." She jerked her thumb over her shoulder.

He massaged her neck. "He may warn you, but that's as far as he's getting. I won't let him get any closer to you, Michelle."

"I trust you." A smile trembled on her lips, and then she ducked away from his touch and rose to her feet. "I'm exhausted. I'm going to bed."

Alone. She didn't say it, but he'd heard it. That one little word on the windshield of her car had torpedoed the growing connection between them.

Maybe Michelle trusted him. But she didn't trust herself.

MICHELLE ROLLED OFF HER sore hip and peered at her alarm clock. She thrust off the covers, swinging her legs over the side of the bed.

Her hands fisted the sheets and she collapsed backward. No school today. The campus had become a crime scene.

She stared at the ceiling and a single tear leaked out of the corner of her eye and ran into her ear. Maybe the killer was punishing women in her class for their sins. Amanda had separated from her husband. Jenny had divorced hers. Belinda had been a stripper.

And she was the daughter of a slut.

She'd have to run that theory by Colin. She covered her face with her hands and expelled a long sigh. His kisses had felt so good last night. So perfect.

Had the killer seen the two of them? Had he been watching their silhouettes at the window?

The thought made her stomach churn. Why was he toying with her? He'd had his opportunities to kill her. Why Amanda first? Being single, she'd been on her own a lot more than Amanda had before her separation from Ryan.

Water splashed in the bathroom sink. Poor Colin—

relegated to a sleeping bag on the carpet again. She'd wanted him in her bed, wanted to feel his strong arms wrapped around her all night…wanted to feel his naked body pressed against hers. But that word on the windshield had created a wedge between them. She couldn't give herself to him completely—not with that word hovering out there in the darkness.

She slid off the bed and switched her pajamas for running clothes and pulled her hair into a ponytail. She poked her head out of her bedroom door and sniffed the air. *Coffee.*

Turning the corner into the living room, she caught her breath. Colin dwarfed her small kitchen as he pulled cups and saucers from her cupboards…shirtless again. Once he'd revealed his scars to her, he couldn't seem to keep his shirt on.

Not that she minded.

"You're not making breakfast again, are you?" She crossed her arms and wedged a shoulder against the fridge. "You're the guest."

He turned with a cup in each hand. "Not guilty. Just getting myself some coffee and heating up some water for tea."

"I don't have school today, so I can make some eggs… unless you're in a hurry."

"I'm in no hurry. I'd like to stick around for the cops and—" he pointed to the laptop "—Alec."

"The scan is done?" Michelle scurried to the kitchen table where her laptop displayed a set of incomprehensible numbers. "What does it all mean?"

"My point exactly. We need Alec to decipher it for us."

"And the cops?"

"I put in a call to remind them. Do you want to go outside and have a look at the car? At least in the light of day we can see what he used to write on the windshield."

She turned her back on the computer and strode into the kitchen. "No need. It was white. I know what he used."

"Oh?"

"White shoe polish." She snagged a tea bag from the tin she kept next to the stove. "Parents use it all the time on their cars to write the names of all-star teams or cheerleading squads going to camp. It's a common practice around here."

"So at least it washes off easily."

Michelle's cell phone rang and she checked the display. "It's my department chair, Mr. Brunswick. Hi, Larry."

"How'd you know it was me?"

"You popped up on my display. You really should use your cell phone more often."

"I'm lucky if I can enter my grades on the computer." He blew out a noisy breath. "Michelle, I'm sorry you were the one who found Jenny."

"I'm sorrier for Jenny."

"Of course. This is terrible. Terrible for our school and our students."

"You haven't heard anything, have you?"

"No, I called to make sure you knew about the schedule for the rest of the week. I know you gave your final exam last month, but other teachers have the option of canceling it for students whose grades won't change one way or the other, or at least making the finals an option for those students who need it to raise their grades."

"Then I'm canceling my quizzes for the week. They were just a little prep for geometry."

"Are you taking care of yourself? Nancy is worried about you. She suggested you stay with us until this blows over."

Michelle glanced at Colin over her shoulder. "I'm okay, Larry. Thank Nancy for me."

She ended the call just as a knock sounded on her front door. She jumped. What didn't make her jump these days?

Dragging his shirt over his head, Colin peered out the window. "Cops, or at least one cop. Your friend from the other night."

Michelle tucked her cell phone in the back pocket of her running shorts and met Jerry at the door. She and Colin trooped out to the car with him.

Jerry asked a few questions, dusted the car for prints and scanned the ground for clues. When he'd left, Colin and Michelle shuffled back into the house none the wiser.

Colin placed a finger beneath her chin and tilted it up. "We didn't expect him to find anything, but at least the CCPD knows you're a target. Now that school is almost at an end, what are the chances of getting away? Did you have vacation planned?"

"Not until later in the summer. After the reunion."

"Are you sure it's still on? After all this?"

"I haven't heard otherwise."

Another knock on the door, another jump. Colin placed his hands on her shoulders. "You need a vacation."

She swayed toward him, warmth suffusing her body. She needed Colin.

As if reading her mind, he brushed her lips with a light kiss. His voice grew husky. "I wanted you last night...in every way."

"Michelle, are you home?"

She broke away from Colin's smoldering blue gaze and opened the door to Alec. "I was going to call you."

"I figured the program finished last night."

"It did."

Alec nodded to Colin. "Roarke."

"Going for a ride?" Colin tipped his head toward Alec's bicycle shorts.

Michelle pinched Colin's backside.

"No school today. Thought I'd check out the results and hit the coast highway." The niceties over, Alec dropped into the chair facing the computer.

He started tapping the keyboard while Michelle returned to the kitchen to make scrambled eggs.

Colin sidled up next to her at the counter and whispered. "Do you want to pinch me again?"

"I will if you don't behave yourself."

Alec called from the next room. "I've isolated the emails, Michelle. Check these out."

Michelle turned down the fire under the pan of eggs, walked toward the table and leaned over Alec's shoulder. She swallowed. "Those are the ones."

"Okay. Give me a few minutes."

Raising her brows at Colin, she returned to the kitchen. She stirred the eggs a few more times and dumped them onto a plate. "Would you like some breakfast, Alec?"

He grunted. "Library."

"Excuse me?"

"The emails. They came from the library."

"Are you kidding?" Michelle dropped the spatula in the pan.

"Nope. The email address at freemail dot com was created on one of the Coral Cove Public Library's computers." He shoved back from the table and held up his hands. "Don't get too excited. It could've been anyone."

Colin took a gulp of his coffee. "And we're going to find him."

COLIN HADN'T WANTED TO leave Michelle alone for the forty-five minutes it took him to go home, shower and change. This sick SOB had Michelle in his sights.

As far as he knew, Amanda hadn't been tormented like

this, nor had the latest victim. It was almost as if the killer had a special interest in Michelle.

But that didn't make sense. She had nothing to do with those other two women, except graduating the same year. That had to be the key. Maybe all these women had turned this guy down in high school, and he was getting his revenge…right before the reunion.

Michelle had been watching for him. As he pulled his car behind hers in the driveway, she slipped out the front door and waved. She'd given up on getting a run in this morning and had changed into a pair of skinny jeans and a light top.

If he'd had a math teacher like Michelle, he wouldn't have been able to concentrate enough to get past two plus two.

She slid into the passenger seat exuding the aroma of flowers—must be her perfume. "How are we going to get any information out of the library? Technically you're not working this case."

"If Britt Lambert is still there, we're in."

Michelle eyed him through narrowed cat eyes. "Britt's still there. Why do you have an in with Britt?"

"She dated my brother."

"Was that before Devon?" Michelle relaxed her shoulders and settled back in her seat, snapping her seat belt.

Was she jealous of his closeness with Britt? A little bit? That had to be a good sign.

"Yeah, Kieran dated Britt before Devon."

Colin experienced the little stab of guilt that always got him when he thought about Kieran's fiancée, Devon Reese. After one brief, awkward, gut-wrenching phone call when he'd returned from Afghanistan without his brother, Colin had never spoken to Devon again.

Couldn't handle talking about his brother with the one person who'd loved Kieran as much as he had.

They pulled into the parking lot and stepped into the air-conditioned silence of the public library.

Michelle nudged him in the ribs and jerked her chin toward the research desk. "We're in luck."

Britt, a pair of glasses shoved on top of her head, was hunched over the counter gossiping with a man—the same man he and Michelle had run into at the restaurant—the father of the young man who'd run off with Michelle's mother.

Colin glanced at Michelle's profile. The man's presence either hadn't registered with her or didn't bother her. Of course, it was the wife who had it in for Michelle.

They hung back until the man, Bob Hastings, smacked the counter and turned, almost bumping into them.

Hastings tripped back a step. "Oops, sorry. Seems like I've been bumping into you all over town, Michelle."

"Careful, Bob." Michelle patted the older man's arm. "Bob, this is Colin Roarke. I didn't have a chance to introduce you the other night."

"I know Colin." He pumped his hand. "Used to play varsity ball with my older son. FBI now, right?"

"That's right."

"Are you here working on these murders?" He shook his head. "Damned creepy. I don't think this town has ever seen anything like it since that girl disappeared at the music festival."

"We'll nail him."

"I hope so." He saluted. "Until the next time we bump into each other, Michelle."

He sauntered off whistling until the librarian at the front desk shushed him.

Colin raised one brow. "Seems like a changed man when he's not with his wife."

"He's okay."

Colin turned back to the research counter and leaned on it. "Hey, Britt."

She spun around. "Colin!"

She stretched out her hands and he took them. "Good to see you. You look great."

"I'd heard you were in town." She switched her attention to Michelle. "I understand you were the one who found Jenny. Are you okay? First Amanda, now Jenny. I didn't even graduate your year and I'm scared to death."

"That's why we're here, Britt." Colin wedged his palms on the counter and hunched his shoulders. "I need to ask you some questions about the computer use in the library."

"Are you working on this case? I didn't even know the FBI was involved. The CCPD hasn't asked me anything yet."

Colin looked in both directions and whispered. "I'm helping out."

Michelle's gaze burned the side of his face, but he kept his eyes on Britt. Maybe he'd get lucky and Michelle would pinch his backside again.

"Really?" Britt's china-blue eyes widened. "What do you need? We have records of the computer usage. Everyone has to sign in before logging into the internet."

Colin exchanged a quick glance with Michelle. "I was hoping you'd say that."

Michelle pulled out the piece of paper on which she'd written the dates and times of the emails and handed it to Colin.

Britt waved her hand. "Follow me around to the office in the back. The records are there."

She ushered them into an office and pulled the blinds over the windows. "Just in case."

She sat in the chair and scooted it in front of the computer monitor. "Okay, what dates are you looking at?"

"Check these out." Colin slid the paper across the desk

blotter, and Britt pulled the glasses off her head and settled them on her nose.

She tapped at the keys, made some notes, tapped again, made more notes. "I think I have your guy, but I don't think he's the killer."

"Who is it?"

"Nick Schaeffer." Britt scribbled the name on the paper and shoved it back to Colin.

"Nick?" Michelle's voice squeaked.

"Who's Nick Schaeffer?"

"H-he's in my class."

Britt clicked her tongue. "You have that little miscreant in your algebra class?"

"He's not so bad."

Colin smacked the piece of paper with his palm. "Yeah, he is. He's been sending you those emails."

Michelle picked up the paper between two fingers and stared at the words as they swung before her. "Are you sure, Britt?"

"He is the only one who signed up to use the computers on those exact dates. Bit of a coincidence."

"Nick can't be the killer. He's fifteen years old, for God's sake."

Britt pushed back from the table. "I agree with you there. He may be a juvenile delinquent, but he's not a killer. So the emails and the murders aren't related."

"School's not in session today, right?" Colin crumpled the piece of paper in his fist. "Let's find Nick and ask him what the hell he was doing sending you those emails."

"You didn't get the info from me." Britt folded her hands on top of the desk. "Especially if you wind up wringing his neck."

As they walked out of the library, Michelle grabbed his

arm. "We can't just march up to his parents' house. With no school and no final exams, he's probably not home, anyway."

"Would it be unusual for you to call him at home, especially under these circumstances? Tell his parents you need to let him know the schedule for the rest of the school year. Find out where he is."

Michelle skimmed a hand through her hair. "I just can't believe Nick would send those messages. He's too young to even know about my mother."

"Can you call him, Michelle?"

"I guess so."

Colin flexed his fingers. What he wanted to do to this boy wasn't far off from Britt's idea. He wanted to teach the punk a lesson.

"I have his home number on my school laptop."

Colin drove back to Michelle's house, and she fired up her work computer. "Here it is."

Colin dug her cell phone from her purse and held it up. "Put it on speaker."

Michelle punched in the boy's number on the phone. "Hello, Mrs. Schaeffer? This is Ms. Girard, Nick's algebra teacher."

"Hello, Ms. Girard. We're in shock over what happened to that counselor and that you found her."

"Yes, it was horrible, so terrible for the students."

"Are you okay?"

"Yes, thank you. I'm calling for Nick, actually. I'm trying to let all my students know about the schedule for this week."

"Well, we got one of those blanket phone messages from the principal. No school today and optional final exams."

"I wanted to let my students know my particular schedule and tell them whether or not they needed to take the quizzes. Is Nick at home?"

"Oh, that's kind of you. The principal's message told the kids to report to school tomorrow for the last day. Nick's at the skate park. I'll give him your message. Does he need to take the quiz?"

Michelle flashed Colin a thumbs-up sign. "No. He has a B in the class and one quiz isn't going to change that."

"Thank you, Ms. Girard. I'll let him know."

"Skate park." Michelle tossed her phone in the general direction of her purse on the counter.

"Can you saunter into the skate park looking for Nick?"

"Not without looking like my mother." Michelle clapped a hand over her mouth, her eyes wide.

Had she just made a joke about her mother robbing the cradle? Colin raised his eyebrows and wiggled them up and down. "Was that a joke?"

"I think it was."

"Good for you." He chucked her under the chin. "So how are you going to casually ask for Nick…without looking like your mother?"

"The skate park's on the edge of Coral Park. We could take a walk there and figure it out as we go along."

Twenty minutes later they were strolling along the sidewalk next to the park, peering through a chain-link fence at helmeted kids careening down slopes and jumping off steps.

Michelle clung to the fence and called to one of the boys. "Noah, come here."

The boy skidded to a stop on his wheels and jogged to the gate. "Ms. Girard?"

"Do you know about the schedule this week? You might want to come in for the quiz since you have a C plus in the class. It could bring up your grade."

"Yeah, if I knew what I was doing. I don't get radical equations."

"Anyone else in there in our class?"

"Uh, no." The kid pushed a tangle of red curls out of his eyes.

"What about Nick Schaeffer? I thought I saw him."

"Nick? Nah, he was here but someone called him on his cell and he took off on his bike." Noah spun around on his board. "Later, Ms. Girard."

Michelle blew out a breath and leaned back, still hanging onto the fence. "Now what?"

"We're going to have to nail him down, Michelle, even if that means bringing in the police."

"I'd rather talk to him first. Nick's not a bad kid. If he sent those emails, there has to be something going on with him."

"You're a great teacher and you have a soft heart, but don't let that blind you to the truth. What he did was wrong and criminal. It's harassment."

She peeled her fingers from the chain link. "I know, but I still want to reach out to him before we call in the cops."

"Too bad you told his mom he didn't have to come to class. You could've pulled him aside after class and asked him then, although I want to be there when you talk to him."

"Now that we're in the park, do you want to take a walk? My brain is scrambled." She rubbed her hands on her jeans. "I still can't believe someone was murdered on campus. Wait until the press descends on us."

He laced his fingers with hers. "Great idea. Let's get some of this fresh ocean air in our lungs and forget about death for a while."

A kid on a bike whizzed past them, yelling.

Colin pointed at him as the boy careened to a stop at the skate park entrance. "Nick?"

"Nope."

The boy hopped off his bike and soon had all the kids bunched around him as he gesticulated and shouted.

Colin tugged on Michelle's hand, veering back toward the skate park. "What happened?"

The boy named Noah turned to face them, his eyes wide and his freckles standing out on his pale face. "Ms. Girard, Nick Schaeffer went off the road on the coast highway."

Chapter Twelve

Michelle shuddered and squeezed Colin's hand. Her voice sliced through the babbling of the boys. "Kyle, is Nick hurt badly?"

Kyle removed his helmet and wiped his forehead with the back of his hand. "I don't know, Ms. Girard. I heard he went off the road and over the edge just past Columbella House."

"Oh, my God."

"Let's go." Colin put his arm around her shoulders. "Let's see what we can find out."

They drove to the end of Coral Cove Drive and turned right onto the coast highway. A swarm of emergency vehicles, their lights revolving in a cavalcade of red and blue, blocked both lanes of traffic.

Colin pulled his car behind a police vehicle. "Is Chief Evans on the scene?"

Michelle squinted at the uniformed people scurrying in and out of the flashing lights. "I don't see him."

"Good." Colin charged out of the car, and Michelle scrambled to keep up with him.

He glommed onto a young officer, Landon Wallis, directing traffic, basically overseeing abrupt U-turns on the other side of the crash site.

"Is the boy okay?"

"He's alive and conscious. They just got him into the ambulance." He nodded to Michelle. "Hey, Michelle. What are you doing here? I swear it's not even a full moon and we're up to our necks in murders and accidents."

"Was it an accident, Landon?" She stepped in front of Colin.

Landon blinked his eyes. "Why wouldn't it be? He's a kid, not a woman with a ten-year reunion coming up."

"I—I mean, did anyone see anything? Did Nick say anything?"

He shrugged and waved at a car slowing down to rubberneck. "I don't know. I'm out here directing traffic."

The ambulance siren whooped a few times and pulled onto the road before accelerating, spewing gravel in its wake.

Turning his back on Landon, Colin zeroed in on the flashing red lights of the ambulance cutting through the rolling fog. "We need to talk to that kid."

"You don't think he found out we were looking for him and tried to harm himself, do you?" She clutched Colin's arm as a wave of nausea washed through her. That's exactly why she hadn't wanted to bring the police into the mix.

"I don't know what to think, Michelle." He covered her hand with his own and led her back to his car. Backing her up against the passenger door, he placed his hands on her shoulders. "But you're going to get us into his hospital room."

"But if he's badly hurt, nobody's going to get in there... and nobody should."

"You heard the cop." He jerked his thumb over his shoulder at Landon still waving his arms like a conductor. "Nick is alive and conscious and he'd better be ready to answer some questions."

MICHELLE'S NOSTRILS FLARED as the antiseptic smell of the hospital washed over her. She hated hospitals. She'd spent too much time in this particular hospital watching Dad die.

Colin jabbed her in the ribs with his elbow. "Are those the parents?"

Michelle nodded as she took in Mr. and Mrs. Schaeffer slumped in a pair of vinyl chairs, foam coffee cups scattered on the table in front of them.

Colin vibrated beside her. He seemed so easygoing on the outside, but a tension coiled inside him ready to spring at the slightest trigger.

She put a hand on the corded muscle of his forearm. "Let me handle this."

Mrs. Schaeffer glanced up from her gossip magazine and offered a weak smile. "Hello, Ms. Girard. It's nice of you to drop by, especially after what you've been through yourself."

Michelle gave Mrs. Schaeffer a one-armed hug and gestured to Colin. "Do you know Colin Roarke?"

Mrs. Schaeffer patted Colin's shoulder. "How are you parents, dear?"

Michelle covered her smile with her hand as a blush touched Colin's cheekbones. "They're just fine, Mrs. Schaeffer. I hope Nick's going to be okay."

Michelle shoved her hands in the pockets of her sweater. "I heard he's going to be fine, right? He just veered off the road. Hello, Mr. Schaeffer."

Nick's dad raised a hand and then closed his eyes again.

"That's Nick's story. He was riding on the edge and his tires slipped." Mrs. Schaeffer's fingers creased the pages of her magazine clutched in her hands.

"You don't believe him?" Michelle's heart thumped in her chest, her fingers curling in her pockets.

"You know how teenaged boys are, Ms. Girard." She raised her eyes to the ceiling as if asking for divine help. "He was probably messing around. Doing something he shouldn't have been doing, like popping wheelies on the edge. We've warned him about that before."

"Is he sleeping now?"

"Yes. Visiting hours are officially over, but the hospital makes allowances for parents."

Mr. Schaeffer opened one eye. "He's just cut and bruised. He's going to be fine. I think we should head home, Sharon."

"What if something happens in the middle of the night?" She plopped back in her chair. "I'm staying right here."

Mr. Schaeffer rose and stretched his arms over his head. "You can stay. I'm heading home to my bed. I'll peek in on him before I leave."

Mrs. Schaeffer sighed and rolled her eyes at Michelle. "Thanks for coming by, Ms. Girard. Nice to see you, Colin."

Michelle and Colin left the waiting room and turned the corner.

Colin placed his lips close to Michelle's ear. "I'm going into the men's room. Hang out here in the corridor and see which room is Nick's."

Colin slipped into the restroom, and Michelle leaned against the wall, flattening her palms behind her.

Mr. and Mrs. Schaeffer shuffled out of the waiting room and headed down the corridor. Three doors from the end of the hallway, they poked their heads into an open room. They disappeared inside and Michelle held her breath.

Colin inched open the bathroom door. "Is it clear?"

"No. They just went into his room."

"Good. It probably means he's still awake."

The door down the hallway swung open, and Michelle put her finger to her lips and took up her position against the wall.

Mr. and Mrs. Schaeffer backed into the corridor, chatting and waving. They continued toward the elevator and when the doors whispered shut, Michelle banged her fist on the men's room door.

"All clear. Hurry, Mrs. Schaeffer must've gone with her

husband to the car, but she'll probably be back for an all-night vigil."

Colin burst through the door. "Show me the way."

She grabbed his hand and their steps echoed in the empty corridor. They reached the door to Nick's hospital room, which the Schaeffers had left ajar, and Colin eased it open.

The TV in the corner cast flickering shadows on the boy in the bed, his head propped on a couple of bunched-up pillows.

His eyes grew big and round as he turned his head toward the door.

"Ms. Girard?"

Colin snapped the door closed behind him, and Michelle approached the bed. "How are you doing, Nick?"

"I—I'm okay."

Michelle dragged a plastic chair to the side of the bed. "I'm glad. What happened?"

Licking his lips, Nick darted a quick look at Colin, blocking the door, his arms crossed over a broad expanse of uncompromising chest.

"I rode my bike off the road. It slid."

She pressed his hand through the sheet. "You have to be careful on that road."

Colin shifted behind her, his voice cutting across the room. "Why did you send those emails to Ms. Girard?"

Nick's face blanched as white as the hospital sheets. "I—I... It's...it's..."

"I was all for turning you in to the cops, but Ms. Girard wants to give you a chance to explain." Colin took two large steps and loomed over Nick's hospital bed. "Explain."

A spasm claimed Nick's battered face, and Michelle held up her hand. "Back off, Colin."

She grabbed a plastic cup with a straw sticking out of it from the bedside table and thrust it at Nick. "We know you sent those emails from the library computer, Nick. Your name's on the record."

Nick lowered his gaze to the cup and he took it from her with a trembling hand. "I'm sorry, Ms. Girard. It was just a joke…a bad joke. I didn't mean anything."

"Bull." Colin smacked a fist into his hand. "What do you know about Ms. Girard's past, anyway?"

"I've heard some stuff." Nick slumped farther into the bed. "Sorry. I stopped when the murders started happening 'cuz I didn't want you to get scared or think the emails had anything to do with the murders…'cuz they didn't."

Michelle folded her hands in her lap and put on her best schoolmarm voice. "I'm disappointed in you, Nick. It was a hurtful prank."

The door swung open and Mrs. Schaeffer stopped short, tilting her head. "What are you doing in Nick's room? Visiting hours are over."

"Oh, I'm sorry, Mrs. Schaeffer." Michelle scooted the chair back and pushed to her feet. "As we were walking by Nick's room, he poked his head out the door. He thought he could catch you before you left. So we just stepped in for a visit. Hope you don't mind."

"Of course not. Did you need something, Nicky?"

"Uh, no. I didn't know if you were leaving with Dad or coming back. That's all."

Michelle smiled at Nick. If he was wondering why his algebra teacher had just lied to his mother and was encouraging *him* to lie to his mother, he didn't show it. He was probably too relieved his algebra teacher hadn't ratted him out.

Michelle nudged Colin, who still looked ready to throttle Nick. They said their goodbyes and get-well-soons and Michelle had to practically push Colin out the door.

He stalked toward the elevator and smacked his palm against the button. "He's lying."

"What do you mean? He's lying about sending the emails or he's lying about it all being a joke?"

"I don't know. Something's not right. The kid was terrified."

Crossing her arms, Michelle tapped her toe. "Why wouldn't he be terrified with you standing over his bed like some crazed drill sergeant?"

"It's more than that, Michelle." He punched the elevator button again for good measure. "He was scared. If it had been a joke, he'd be more defensive or more ashamed—not petrified."

The doors of the elevator whisked open and Colin proceeded to do violence to the buttons inside the car. Michelle grabbed his hand before he started another assault. "What is it you think is going on?"

"I'm not sure. Why did he have that accident just when we'd discovered he was the one sending those emails to you? It's too much of a coincidence."

"You think his accident has something to do with the emails?"

"Maybe he's not the only one involved. Maybe there were others, and they wanted Nick to take the rap."

"I don't know. I'm just glad we discovered who was doing it and that it's not related to the murders."

"Who says?"

The elevator doors opened onto the second parking level and Michelle hugged her sweater around her body against the cool sea breeze. "You can't believe that teen in the hospital bed had anything to do with the murders."

"It's all tied together—the emails, Nick's accident, the murders. When something looks like a coincidence, it usually isn't."

Michelle shivered. "You're scaring me."

Colin blew out a breath and draped an arm around her shoulders. "I'm sorry. I want this to be over for you, and I want to bring it to an end before my vacation is over and the FBI sends me out on a case."

With visiting hours at an end and most of the hospital staff gone for the day, Colin's rental car had a row to itself. Colin hit the remote and the car beeped once. He got the door for her and Michelle slid onto the seat, glancing over her shoulder. She tugged her sweater around her more tightly.

Colin eased the car into the foggy night and clicked on his brights.

Michelle peered out the window. "I hope we see more sun when July rolls around. This has been one of the most overcast summers in a while."

"The sun peeks out for an hour or two in the afternoon and the gray stuff starts swirling in from the ocean."

"It's going to be strange at school tomorrow. I'm sure everyone's going to be talking about the murder and not much else. Maybe Mr. Ochoa should've canceled the rest of the school year."

"Kids still have to graduate, right? When is that?"

"Graduation is on Friday night."

Colin veered onto the coast highway, back toward Coral Cove. A few cars crawled past them in the fog. Had to be locals traveling from one coastal town to the other. Tourists always plowed through the mist too fast, not realizing the density could change with every hairpin turn.

Colin's car picked up speed downhill, and he hugged the shoulder of the road. Another car whizzed past them on the left, venturing across the double yellow line to pass them.

"Idiot." Colin flashed his brights at the back-end of the car.

"Has to be an outsider. No central coast resident in his right mind would pass on a night like this."

"I hope he's not staying in Coral Cove." Colin drummed his fingers on the steering wheel. "The cops didn't say anything about skid marks near where Nick went over the edge, did they?"

"Now what are you driving at? You think some car forced Nick's bike off the road?"

"Maybe."

"But why would he lie about that? Seems to me that scenario gets him off the hook."

"Or maybe another bike forced him off."

"Another bike?" Michelle sucked in a breath. "You're not still thinking Alec Wright has something to do with the emails, are you? He's the one who directed us to the library's computers."

"Yeah, why did he do that? So we'd discover Nick's involvement?"

"You're crazy. No way." She clutched the edge of the seat as the car took the next turn. "Slow down. You're as bad as that other guy."

Colin's downhill speed picked up on the straightaway, and Michelle glanced at him. His hands gripped the wheel as he pumped the brakes. "Colin, slow down."

"I'd love to, sweetheart, but we have no brakes."

Chapter Thirteen

Colin cursed and pumped the brakes again. He tried the parking brake, but it wouldn't catch. The car tunneled forward, sightless, into the unknown. He cranked the steering wheel to the right, and the tires crunched gravel and dirt.

Michelle gasped and gripped the armrest.

"Hang on, Michelle." Colin gritted his teeth and took the next turn at a wide angle. Headlights pinned them in the oncoming traffic lane, and Colin swerved back inside, grazing the guardrail on the passenger side. The long blare of a horn echoed as the other car zoomed past them.

"I'm going to turn off the engine and try to make it to the next turnout, the view point just before Columbella House."

"That's a sheer drop-off if you go through the guardrail."

"We'll just have to make sure we don't go through the guardrail." He cranked off the engine and threw the car into Park. The vehicle lurched and whined.

Colin guided it around the next bend in the road, and it shuddered but the action slowed the car's careening downhill course. He knew this road like the back of his hand. One more stretch of straightaway and then he could aim the car toward the large turnout that offered spectacular views of California's central coast…a view he'd rather take in from the top than the bottom.

Light filled the car from behind as another car rode up

on their tail. Colin glanced down at the speedometer, which ticked down another five miles an hour.

"Take off your seat belt, Michelle."

She turned a pair of wide, glassy eyes on him. "Are you nuts?"

"The car's slowing down, but it still might be going fast enough to crash through that guardrail. We have room in the turnout to jump out of the car before it hits the guardrail."

Michelle unsnapped her seat belt and shifted her right hand to the door handle. "Are you going to tell me if and when I need to jump?"

"Yep."

The car continued its silent journey through the fog, no longer picking up speed as the road leveled out. Colin spotted the beginning of the turnout and cranked the steering wheel to the left, praying for no oncoming traffic.

He steered the car into the turnout where it hissed over the gravel. He continued his struggle with the steering wheel to take the car around the curve instead of straight toward the edge. The car fought him, but the tires churned the gravel on the turn.

His hand clammy, Colin gripped the door handle. The guardrail loomed ahead.

"Jump!"

After making sure Michelle had her door open, Colin shoved open the driver's-side door and hurled himself to the ground. He rolled a few feet and smacked against the guardrail.

A loud bang and some screeching of metal on metal made him grind his teeth together. With his heart racing faster than that runaway car, he lurched to his hands and knees and scanned the fog-shrouded lookout area.

A dark shape huddled in the mist and Colin scrambled across the dirt and gravel in the direction of the moaning.

Michelle lay on her side, propped up on one forearm. Colin crouched beside her. "Are you okay?"

Twisting her head, she pointed toward the cliff edge. The rental car had smashed against the guardrail, bending the metal out toward the ocean. The front wheels were still spinning and hanging over the edge of the precipice.

"We may have jumped out just in time." She ended on a moan and clutched her arm.

Colin crawled behind her and pulled her against his chest. He buried his face in her hair, which smelled of oil and dust. He wrapped his arm around her midsection and her heart hammered against his arm.

"Are you hurt?"

"I landed on my side and ate dirt. I'm going to be sore all over tomorrow, but I think I'm in one piece. How about you?"

"My back smashed into the guardrail. I don't think I'll be running a marathon anytime soon, but I'll live."

"What just happened?"

"Someone tampered with my brakes."

She shuddered in his arms, and he kissed the side of her neck. "I have my cell in my pocket."

"Someone knew we were visiting Nick. You were right. There's more to Nick's story."

"And we're definitely not getting it from him now." Colin placed a call to 9-1-1 and gave their details to the emergency operator.

"Can you stand up now?" Colin hooked his arms beneath Michelle's.

"Sure." She leaned against him and dug her heels into the gravel where they slipped beneath her. "With a little help."

"Don't worry. I've got you." He steadied her and lifted her to her feet. When she hit solid ground she pulled away, but he crushed her against his chest.

He never wanted to let go.

"When the school term is over, you need to leave, Michelle. You're not safe in Coral Cove."

"And what about you?" She jerked her arm toward his rental car crumpled against the guardrail. "That accident targeted both of us...and you graduated four years before I did."

"When I go back to work, I'm not going to be assigned to this case. Once the police agencies make an official connection between these murders and the ones in Vegas and San Francisco, the FBI will send in a team for this area. That's not me."

"So what's your interest?"

"You." He brushed a strand of hair from her cheek. "You're my interest...and seeing you safe."

Her long, dark lashes fluttered and her lips parted. Colin bent his head and touched his mouth to hers. He didn't know if the gritty sand that roughened their kiss came from him or her, and he didn't care.

The wail of a siren made them jump apart, but Colin kept Michelle in his arms.

She had to leave, but sending her away from a killer meant sending her away from him, too. And he had no intention of losing Michelle.

MICHELLE DABBED SOME antibiotic cream on the small cut on her chin and studied herself in the mirror. Her nice, soft bed beckoned and Colin had to bunk on the floor...again. After flinging himself out of a moving car.

Her gaze shifted to the bed in the reflection. Big enough for two.

She pulled her hair back and drew closer to the mirror, studying her features. Her mother's daughter in every way.

No. Not in every way. Colin wasn't some impressionable teenage boy ready to be seduced by Mrs. Robinson.

He was a man who'd been doing his level best to protect her. He cared about her. His eyes changed when he looked at her. The sadness dropped away. He almost seemed like the carefree boy she'd admired from afar in high school.

She did that for him. It wasn't the stuff of her dreams.

She'd wasted too much time worrying about what other people thought of her. After she'd spent that summer in France, she vowed never to allow that to happen again.

She was no slut like her mother. Maybe her mother didn't even deserve that epithet.

Michelle was a woman who cared about a man. A man she might never see again once she left town for someplace safe. And where was that? She'd never felt safer than she did in Colin's warm embrace...even with a killer on the loose.

She blew out a breath, fogging up the mirror, and pulled the elastic out of her hair. Shaking her hair out around her shoulders, she moistened her lips.

She was a woman who wanted her man.

With butterflies in her belly, Michelle edged around the corner of the hallway. She braced her hand against the wall and leaned forward.

Colin lay stretched out on the floor, encased in the sleeping bag, his head propped up by two pillows bunched beneath it. The TV emitted a low murmur punctuated by gunshots.

Colin lifted his head and hoisted himself up on his elbows. "Is it too loud? It was fine until they started shooting."

"Isn't it always?"

"Huh?"

The blue glow from the TV washing over his body, his

bare chest, made him look otherworldly, like a strange crea-
ture from a strange land. It gave her confidence.

She prowled toward him, her body sensitive wherever her
nightgown brushed her skin. She continued across the sleeping bag until she stood, straddling it. She placed her hands
on her hips and felt like an Amazon woman. Sure of herself
and her mission.

Leaning back farther, Colin assessed her through half-
closed eyes. "Did you forget something?"

"Yeah, I did."

She lowered her body until her knees pinned the sleeping
bag on either side of his legs. She gritted her teeth against the
soreness that assaulted just about every inch of her frame,
and forced the grimace into her most seductive smile.

Colin's eyes kindled as he deliberately dropped his gaze
from her face to her breasts. The look reached out to her like
a touch, and tingles of desire showered through her body,
puddling in all the right spots.

Her heart thudded with sweet anticipation but Colin lay
still, his hands curling into the folds of the sleeping bag. He
was going to make her do all the work? Snagging her lower
lip between her teeth, she landed on his thighs.

"Ouch!" He sat up, facing her. "I just took a tumble out
of a moving car, remember?"

"Sorry. I'm supposed to be…to be… And here I am torturing you. No, not torturing you…" She clapped a hand over
her mouth. How could she call this torture when the man
had been through real torture? And he had the scars on his
chest to prove it.

Colin reached up and peeled the hand from her face.
"What do you want, Michelle?"

She wanted for once not to worry about labels, about
being judged, about the shadow of her mother's mistakes.

"I want you." Her fingers trailed from the edge of the

sleeping bag around Colin's waist up his taut belly to the hard planes of his chest. She flattened her palms against his pecs and stretched so that her head rested against his hip bone.

She turned her head and laid a path of kisses that followed the same journey as her fingertips. Her hair skimmed his torso, and she felt him shift beneath her. Sitting up, she scooted from his thighs to his crotch.

He sucked in a breath.

"Does that hurt?"

"In all the right places." He grinned and cinched her waist with his big hands.

The power of her womanhood thrilled her. It was a power she hadn't exercised much over the years—too frightened, too restricted...too stupid.

She eased forward, clamping her thighs along his hips. She steadied her hands against his broad shoulders and kissed his mouth. Tentative. Sweet.

He sealed his lips with hers, invading her mouth with his tongue. Demanding. Hot.

Sighing into his kiss, she collapsed on top of his body. She didn't know if she'd hurt all his sore places or not, but she no longer had the strength to hold herself upright. The heat of his flesh scorched her through the thin cotton of her nightgown.

He deepened the kiss, as if her total surrender hadn't been enough for him. His rough hands plowed beneath her nightgown, rasping against the skin of her back. He tucked the edges of his fingers in the elastic of her panties, caressing the beginning curve of her derrière.

He murmured against her mouth. "How am I supposed to get these off with you sitting on me?"

"Hmm?" The absence of his lips from hers had left a void.

She nibbled on his lower lip to fill it. His kiss had intoxicated her. Could a person get drunk on pleasure?

"These?" His fingers twisted the material of her panties. "Lift up so I can take them off…because I have every intention of taking them off this time."

The threads of electricity that tingled up her thighs at his intimate touch zapped her out of her languorous stupor. She drove her knees into his sides, and he grunted.

"Now *that* hurt."

"I'm not much of a seductress, am I?"

"You—" he sat up and gripped the hem of her nightgown "—have—" he bunched the material in his hands "—no—" he yanked it up and over her head "—idea."

The cool air that flashed across her skin pebbled her nipples. Or had Colin's touch done that? In seconds, he replaced that coolness with warmth as his lips closed around one tight and aching nipple.

She arched her back, inviting him to explore farther. And he did. His tongued dabbled at one breast and then the other. His hand molded her flesh for his delight.

She clutched at his thick, wavy hair, urging him on to a task that he performed with relish. She wanted him right here in this sleeping bag.

"Wait!"

He froze, his head buried between her breasts. His muffled words blew hot against her chest. "You want to stop? Now?"

"No." She combed his hair into curls around her fingers. "I want this to go on and on and on—in the bedroom. That's why I came out here, to rescue you from the floor."

"How often do I get to have a woman in a sleeping bag?" He kissed the tip of her breast and she shivered.

"How often?"

"Never." He bucked her off his body and unzipped the bag. "Come on in."

She shimmied closer to the puffy softness of the sleeping bag and he placed a hand on her belly. "One rule. You have to be naked to enter."

Her stomach fluttered beneath his hand, and she hooked her thumbs around the elastic of her panties and peeled them off.

His blue eyes darkened to indigo as he drank in her bare flesh.

She peeled back a corner of the sleeping bag and peeked inside. His erection was apparent beneath his briefs, and she swallowed. "You, too."

In a flash, he slipped out of his briefs and threw them over his shoulder. "I always follow the rules."

He pulled her down next to him, and their bodies met along every line. Michelle could've sworn she heard a sizzle as skin met skin. He dragged her into one of those bone-melting kisses, and their bodies fused together like one entity.

As Colin zipped them into a cocoon of warmth, Michelle clung to him. She'd never felt so safe with a man in her life. And when he left, she'd never feel that way again.

Their kisses and their touches became hungry, desperate, seeking a reassurance for the mind only the body could give. When they joined together, Michelle took in every part of him—the sadness, the regret, the guilt. She wanted him to purge it all.

And her fears and hang-ups? She felt only love.

When they lay side by side, sated, Colin traced a line up her throat to her lips. "That was the best seduction I've had in a long time."

"Really?" She smiled and kissed his finger.

"I think you should practice on me all the time."

She hoisted up on one elbow. "You mean for the next few days, until you pack me up and run me out of town."

"I don't want to push you away, Michelle, but I do want to keep you safe. I have to keep you safe." The line of his jaw hardened and old hurts haunted his eyes.

She took his face in her hands. "You've done more to protect me in the past few days than anyone has ever done in my entire lifetime."

"And I'm not going to stop now. Someone almost killed both of us tonight. He's not going to quit until he gets what he wants."

"Okay, I'll go away." She ran the pads of her thumbs across his cheekbones. "And when it's all over? When the FBI or Coral Cove P.D. or the county sheriffs bring this guy down…?"

He crushed her hands in his. "I'll come and get you, Michelle."

His vehemence prodded that little niggling doubt in the back of her head. "Will it be the same for us? For you?"

"Why would it be any different?"

She glanced away from his eyes, kindling with emotions he wouldn't acknowledge. "Once this killer is behind bars and I'm safe, I won't need your protection anymore. I won't need you to save me at every turn. Will it be the same…for you?"

He squeezed her hands once, almost painfully, before he dropped them. "Is that what you think? You believe my attraction for you is based on my need to protect you?"

"Is it?"

She held her breath. The seconds ticking by dragged like hours. The pent-up air burned her lungs.

The lines on Colin's face softened, the furrow between his eyebrows smoothed out. "I don't think so. Is that good enough for right now?"

The storm in his eyes had blown over. He'd answered her as honestly as he could, and it had to be good enough for now. Because now was all they had.

She nodded, her bottom lip quivering like a baby's. Colin stopped the quivering with a hard kiss to her mouth.

"What we just did in this sleeping bag?" He plucked at the downy folds of their makeshift love nest. "It didn't feel like protection to me."

She twisted her lips into a smile. Of course it didn't. He was a man. Sex felt like...sex. But to her, the fierce tenderness with which he'd taken her had felt like a cotton-wrapped dream.

Sighing, she wiggled her toes against his shins. "You may have grown accustomed to sleeping on the floor in a sleeping bag, but I'm going to insist you move to the bed. We're all ginned up on ibuprofen now, but wait until morning hits us like a sledgehammer."

"If you take me to your bed, are you going to take advantage of me there, too?"

"If you're lucky."

He ran his hand up her back and caressed her neck. "Mmm, I feel lucky."

If Colin continued in this vein, they'd never get out of this sleeping bag. "Water?" She flipped back the sleeping bag and struggled to her feet.

"You go warm the bed. I'll get the water."

Michelle spun around and froze. With knees trembling, she dropped to their makeshift bed.

"Colin, there's someone at the window."

Chapter Fourteen

The fog of desire that had encased his brain dissipated in an instant. The adrenaline that had fueled his hunger for Michelle now raced for a different reason.

He kicked at the sleeping bag twisted around his legs and cursed. Finally stumbling to his feet, he lurched for his weapon resting uselessly on the kitchen table. He clicked off the safety and charged the front door.

"You're naked!"

"Doesn't mean I can't shoot the SOB playing peeping Tom."

He threw open the door and stared blindly into the swirling fog, one streetlight acting as a beacon in the mist. He cursed again. "Doesn't this town know it's summer?"

Michelle pressed in behind him, shoving his jeans into his back. "Since you have your gun, let's take a look outside, but you can't go out there like that."

She'd snatched a robe from somewhere, covering up all her delectably smooth skin—the smooth skin some lunatic had been ogling through a hitch in the curtains.

Colin stepped into his jeans while Michelle claimed a flashlight by the door. "You keep the flashlight. I'll carry the gun."

The moist air settled on his heated flesh and steam rose from his body. He launched off the front step and trudged through Michelle's flower bed to get close to the window. He ran his hand along the damp glass. "No cameras this time."

The beam from the flashlight jerked as Michelle sucked in a breath. "I didn't even think of that."

Colin crept out of the flowers, taking a few with him between his toes. As he slogged through the front lawn toward the sidewalk, the dew from the grass soaked the hem of his jeans. Michelle's front gate hung open as if taunting them: *I let him in and I let him out again.*

"I don't get it." Colin shoved the gate and it clattered against the fence. "How does he get away so fast? There's no sound of an engine. He has to live nearby."

Michelle grabbed the swinging door, silencing the creaking hinges. "The cops questioned everyone on this block the night of Amanda's murder. Nobody raised any red flags and nobody noticed anyone crashing through their backyards that night. It's like he melts into the fog."

Colin's gaze swept the street. The vacationing neighbors' porch light glowed across the way. He continued scanning the gray muck that shifted before his eyes. The guy could be standing fifty feet away and they'd have trouble figuring out if he were a man or a tree.

"Colin!" Michelle clutched his arm, her short fingernails digging into his skin. "I saw a flickering light at Columbella. I swear."

He peered at the dark, hulking shape, which crouched on the cliff's edge like a menacing beast. Every line and plane of the house exuded darkness. He recalled the lurking peril he'd felt in the basement, a palpable thing that tasted and smelled like…death.

"I don't see anything."

She puffed out a breath beside him. "It's gone now, but I saw it—just for a moment, a flicker like the bouncing beam of a flashlight." With her own flashlight, she emulated what she'd seen.

"The CCPD released Chris Jeffers yesterday, after the Procter murder. Did they run him out of town, or did he slip back into his free digs?"

"You think it's Chris?" She huddled in next to him, and he curled his arm around her back, tucking his hand beneath the belt of her robe. "Or do you think I imagined it?"

He planted a kiss on her cool temple. "You're too practical for wild imaginings. If you saw something, I believe you."

"Then we need to investigate." Her back straightened as if her spine had turned into a rod of steel.

Colin secured the safety on his weapon and tucked it into the waist of his jeans. "Let me grab a shirt before I freeze to death."

"Don't say that." Michelle grabbed him around the middle and squeezed the breath out of him…and he didn't mind at all.

They returned inside, pulled on more appropriate clothing for skulking around an old house, and locked up behind them.

"I'm betting nobody boarded up that window on the kitchen door." Colin held open the side gate for Michelle and they shuffled along the side of the house, the light from the flashlight illuminating the uneven ground.

"You should take your luck to Vegas." She waved her hand through the hole in the window.

More of the pieces had been knocked out, and Colin had an even easier time reaching his arm between the jagged pieces of glass to unlock the kitchen door.

Once again they slipped into the kitchen, but this time there was no daylight to brighten the room. They tiptoed across the tiled floor.

Michelle tugged at his pocket and put her finger to her lips. She cocked her head.

Colin held his breath, and then he heard it. A soft, snuffling sound. A hiccup. A sniffle.

He tracked the sound around the corner from the kitchen. God, don't let it be coming from the basement. Not that the basement scared him or anything...

He turned the corner with Michelle beside him. For some reason, she killed the flashlight and Colin tripped over a piece of furniture. Something or someone sucked in a breath, and then a dark shape loomed before them.

The adrenaline pumping through his blood at double time, Colin coiled his muscles and then launched himself into the air like he was aiming for the end zone after a fifty-yard sprint. He extended his arms for the tackle and brought down...a girl.

COLIN GRUNTED AS HE made contact with the intruder, who answered with a squeal. Michelle thumbed on the flashlight, aiming the spear of light at the two figures tangled on the floor. "Did you get him? Did you get him?"

The glow from the flashlight picked out a swath of gleaming blond hair spread on the floor. Michelle hunched forward and stalked toward Colin and his prey.

As she drew closer, the light encircled Colin as he hauled up his quarry to a sitting position. Michelle dropped the flashlight and it landed on a coffee table, pointing right at the duo on the floor.

"Maddie?"

"You know this girl?" Colin swept a curtain of yellow hair from Maddie's face, damp with tears.

"Y-yes, of course I know Maddie. She's in one of my classes." Michelle crouched next to the girl who choked back a sob. "What are you doing here, Maddie? Are you all right?"

The girl shook her head, her straight hair falling over her face again. "I'm worried about Nick, Ms. Girard."

"Of course." Michelle shot a glance at Colin, who'd backed off and now sat on the floor, his back against an overstuffed chair. "You're still dating him, aren't you?"

Although the action was impossible, Michelle could sense Colin pricking up his ears at the mention of Nick Schaeffer.

Maddie sniffled and dipped her head.

"I saw him earlier. He's going to be fine."

"It was so scary. He could've died."

"But he didn't."

"When I told my mom what happened, she got mad. She told me I should stop dating Nick because he's trouble, but he's not, Ms. Girard. Is he?"

Maddie's eyes glinted between the strands of her hair. Did she know what her boyfriend had been up to with the emails?

"Nick's an okay kid."

Colin's hand shot out and grabbed the flashlight. He beamed it into Maddie's face. "You didn't answer Ms. Girard's first question. What are you doing here?"

Maddie's eyes widened, and she looked like a deer caught in the…flashlight. "Wh-when I got in that fight with my mom, I just wanted to leave the house. This place, Columbella House, is special to me and Nick. So I wanted to come here."

"Were you at Ms. Girard's house earlier?"

Maddie peeking into her window in the middle of the night? Ludicrous. Colin was losing it. He must not trust kids.

"No." Maddie pushed her hair behind her ears. "Why would I go there? I headed straight to Columbella."

"Did you see anyone on the street?" Colin was using that flashlight like he was conducting an inquisition. "Did you notice anyone near Ms. Girard's house tonight?"

"No." Maddie's eyes, her pupils dilated, darted toward Michelle.

"You shouldn't be out and about at this time of night, Maddie. It's dangerous. There have already been two murders in this town."

"I don't have to worry about the Reunion Killer, Ms. Girard."

The Reunion Killer? They'd already given him his very own name? "Everyone should be concerned, Maddie. Why do you think you don't have to worry about him?"

Maddie shrugged. "I didn't graduate ten years ago."

COLIN PULLED MICHELLE close and she rested her cheek against his thudding heart. "Did you believe her?"

"I don't trust any of these kids."

"I can't imagine Maddie as our peeping Tom."

He drummed his fingers against the curve of her hip. "Just like you couldn't imagine Nick sending those emails. You're too soft, Ms. Girard."

The pressure of his fingers lightened and the taps turned into swirls. "You're very soft, Ms. Girard."

She snuggled against his hard body, which felt more comfortable than the plushest bed on earth. She didn't care about the taunting emails or the word scrawled on the windshield of her car. She didn't care about Marybeth Hastings's cold shoulder.

She had her man, and she didn't intend on losing one precious minute of their time together.

The following morning, Michelle regretted those precious minutes she'd spent with Colin last night…but only until the time it took her to hit the shower and turn her sleepy face toward the warm spray of the water.

Only one more day to get through, and she planned to spend most of the day inputting the rest of the scores and giving quizzes to those students who needed to bring up their grades.

Then she'd get out of Dodge.

The reunion committee was piling up cancellations at a rapid rate. There was no need for the CCPD to warn the women of her graduating class about the danger that lurked in Coral Cove. Anyone who was still local knew exactly who had the bull's-eye on their backs.

And Michelle felt hers growing bigger every day.

She floated her tea bag on top of the water and Colin sauntered into the kitchen with a towel low on his hips, looking ten to the third power sexy. She stood there dunking her tea bag in and out of the boiling water with what she knew was a goofy grin on her face, drinking in the total package in front of her.

He cocked one eyebrow at her and his sexiness climbed to the tenth power.

Leveling a finger at her cup, he said, "I think you'd better leave that tea bag in the water for a few minutes instead of dipping it in and out."

Her hand trembled and a little hot water splashed her fingers. "Oops." She set the cup down on the counter, and Colin was at her side in a second with a dish towel.

"Did you burn yourself?"

"No." She sucked her fingers into her mouth and Colin's gaze followed the action, his eyes igniting with an inner flame like a blue pilot light.

Shaking her head, she ran her fingers under the cool tap water. "I hope I didn't wake you. I thought you might want to sleep in."

"The bed felt empty."

Oh, boy. How was she supposed to leave Coral Cove… and this man?

"I have to leave for school." She waved her hand vaguely around the kitchen. "Help yourself."

"I will." He made a move and pinned her against the sink, his kiss like an assault on all her senses.

She surrendered—for just a moment. Placing her hands against his granite chest, she shoved. "I have to get to school. Last day."

"Thank God for that." He balanced his hands on her shoulders. "How do you feel? Is your body as sore as mine? I mean from the car accident."

Michelle's cheeks heated. She'd never been one for sexual banter or double entendre. It usually made her uncomfortable, but Colin's comment, coupled with the pressure of his strong fingers on her shoulders, sent flutters to her belly and lower...not uncomfortable at all.

"I was stiff this morning." Seeing the smile tug at Colin's lips, she placed her fingers against his mouth. "Don't even go there."

He kissed her hand. "You need to go off to school and be a proper example for your students."

"And you? What are you going to do today?"

"I'm going to nose around the police station and see if I can discover if they culled any evidence from the second murder site. They're playing it very close to the vest. I might even drop in on Nick Schaeffer to see if he has anything to add to his girlfriend's story."

"Stay away from Nick. He's afraid of you, anyway. He won't tell you a thing."

"You're right. I'll stick to the cops, and then we'll grab some dinner. Those sandwiches we gobbled up before visiting Nick in the hospital didn't cut it."

Michelle scooted past Colin and slid her purse from the back of a chair. "I can't do dinner. I'm sorry, I forgot to tell you. Larry Brunswick and his wife have a get-together at their house on the last day of school every year for the math department."

"Even this year, with all this stuff going on?"

"Especially this year. You can come if you like."

"I think I'll pass." He snagged her bag from the corner and hitched it over her shoulder. "But call me when you're done over there, and I'll pick you up or walk you home or something. I don't want you wandering the streets alone."

"I won't be doing that."

He kissed her hard as if imprinting his stamp on her lips.

Michelle swung into the school parking lot with ropes of tension knotted in her stomach. A police car was stationed on the street in front of the school office and clutches of students were scattered across the quad. The murder of Ms. Procter had cast a pall over the typical hustle-bustle of the morning school rituals—a pall as gray and damp as the persistent marine layer.

This was going to be one strange day.

WHEN COLIN GOT OUT OF the shower, he pulled on his clothes from yesterday. The hem of his jeans was still damp from the nighttime excursion to Columbella House.

Why had that girl chosen a spooky old house for refuge?

Of course, his brother, Kieran, had always had a thing for that house. He and his girlfriend, Devon. They'd used it as a rendezvous. Maybe Nick and Maddie had used it for the same purpose.

He carried his coffee to the couch and settled against a soft cushion. Leaning forward, he reached for the remote, sliding it from a large, slick book with a dolphin on the cover.

He recognized that dolphin. He dropped the remote and scooped up the book from the table. Michelle must've dragged out her yearbook, after all.

He thumbed through the pages, and the smell of old glue wafted from the book. His fingertips skimmed across the glossy pages of smiling faces, wedging at the section for senior pictures.

Tiffany. Belinda. Amanda. Jenny.

The girls' bright faces all shone with hope. Now they were dead. Why? Why these four girls? Why Michelle? There were other girls from this class and they hadn't been threatened…yet.

He turned to the front of the book. Michelle didn't have many signatures. She had just about the same number of faculty signatures as classmates'. Even Mr. Brunswick had scrawled a good luck message to Michelle in the corner of his faculty picture. Reading the messages seemed like prying.

He continued to shuffle through the pages, studying the club photos, the sports shots and the candid pictures around campus. Michelle showed up in a few of the group photos— chess club, Spanish club, National Honors Society. No cheerleading or homecoming princessing for Michelle Girard.

Although she could shake his pom-poms any day.

He slurped his lukewarm coffee and balanced the book on his knees for a closer inspection. Amanda showing some leg in the quad with a gaggle of other girls—a pretty girl who'd turned into an attractive woman—an attractive, dead woman.

His pulse ticked up a few notches. He brought the book close to his face and zeroed in on that group of leggy girls. Tiffany. Belinda. Amanda. Jenny. And another girl he didn't recognize. But no Michelle.

She didn't belong in that picture of popular girls. Why did she belong with them now…on a killer's list?

He shook out a perfume card from a magazine on the table and shoved it into the book to mark that page. Then he shuffled back to the senior pictures and studied the faces of each girl.

He flipped back and forth between the group picture and the individual portraits to locate that fifth girl. After several minutes, he released a frustrated breath. The girls looked different in their senior pictures—fancy hair, makeup, the black dress.

He snapped his fingers and cruised to the cheerleading photos. He couldn't locate Belinda, but the other three smiled and high-kicked their way through several shots. He noted a girl that could be match for the one in the group photo— Amy Veracruz.

He'd found a connection between the murdered women, but what about Michelle? It didn't make sense. If some disgruntled high school geek turned psycho adult wanted to off all the girls who'd dissed him in high school, adding to his teenage angst, why had this weirdo added Michelle to his list?

Had the guy mistaken Michelle's shyness for rejection? Or maybe he'd figured he had a chance with a fellow geek and Michelle shot him down—not out of cruelty but the fear of her own sexuality. The killer wouldn't make any distinction.

Colin ran his index finger across the senior pictures again, focusing on the boys this time. He jotted down the names of a few likely candidates when he stumbled across a photo of a fair-haired boy with serious eyes behind a pair of thick glasses. Alec Wright.

Michelle hadn't mentioned that Alec had been in her class.

Colin upended the book from his lap and paced to the window, checking his watch. Michelle had a short schedule today, and then planned to stay at school to finish grading.

But she needed to eat lunch and he knew for a fact she hadn't packed one.

He tucked the yearbook under his arm. He'd head home, put on a change of clothes and then he and Michelle were going for a walk down memory lane.

MICHELLE SQUEEZED HER eyes shut and pinched the bridge of her nose. The tension had hung over the school like a storm waiting to break. Most of her students hadn't bothered showing up to class, satisfied with the grade they already had or maybe just too spooked to walk into a crime scene.

She grabbed the file folder for first period algebra and logged on to the grading website. Thank goodness for computers and these websites that calculated the final grades for teachers.

Sue Daniels poked her head into the classroom and Michelle jumped.

Sue clapped a hand over her mouth. "Sorry. Didn't mean to scare you. I think everyone's on edge today. I'm just glad the school year is over."

"Almost over." Michelle pointed to her laptop. "Are you going to Larry's annual end-of-the-school-year bash?"

"Yeah, I think I'll mosey on over there. I need a drink like nobody's business." Sue winked. "You should try it sometime."

Sue glanced into the hallway, her eyes widening. "Hello, handsome. You need a quick course in geometry?"

Colin's low laugh rumbled outside the door, and the sound made Michelle's mouth water.

He squeezed his big frame past Sue and sauntered into Michelle's classroom. "I try to use geometry as little as possible."

"Too bad." Sue winked at Michelle. "I take it back. You don't need a drink. You've got something a lot better."

As she left, Colin raised his brows. "Did I miss something? Have you taken up drinking now?"

"No, unless you're offering a soda—" she stood up and stretched "—something with lots of caffeine."

"I'm offering you a lunch break with as much caffeinated soda as you like." He waved a book in the air. "But it's a working lunch."

She noticed the blue dolphin on the cover of the book. "You found my yearbook."

"Did you have a chance to look at it when you took it out?"

"No. Did you find something?"

Colin glanced over his shoulder. "Yeah, I did. Let's discuss it at lunch. We'll even go to that healthy place you like."

After Michelle locked up her classroom, they took a drive to The Great Earth down the street from the high school. The noon crowd had already dispersed, so they had a window table in the corner all to themselves.

They ordered their food and Colin plunked the book in front of Michelle. "I found a candid picture with all four victims and a fifth girl. I think it's Amy Veracruz."

He flipped open the book where he'd marked a page and stabbed a finger at a picture of five girls in the quad, all trying for seductive poses.

Michelle's nose stung as she traced her fingertip around Amanda's young face. Her gaze shifted to the other girls and she named them off. "Belinda, Tiffany, Jenny and Amy Veracruz."

The name brought a sour taste and a twist to Michelle's lips.

Colin didn't miss a thing. "Not your best friend, I take it?"

"Amy Veracruz was a witch." She grabbed her soda and

took a long swig. "Not that I should be speaking ill of the dead."

Colin's mouth dropped open. "She was murdered, too?"

"No." Michelle waited for the waitress to put their plates on the table. "She died in a car accident a few years after graduation."

"So he doesn't need to kill her." Colin tapped the picture. "Here's our connection, Michelle. All of these girls were murdered. Every one of them, except Amy, who died too soon."

"You're forgetting one thing."

"You."

"I didn't have anything to do with those girls in high school—totally different cliques, totally different activities. It's not like that horror movie. Nobody knew what we did last summer because we didn't do anything in the summer together."

Colin busied himself with his burger, not meeting her eyes. "What about boys?"

"Boys? You're kidding, right? I didn't date in high school."

"You didn't date but that doesn't mean you weren't asked out. Did you shoot someone down?"

She stabbed a piece of lettuce with her fork. "Nobody asked me out, Colin."

"Stupid teenage boys." He smoothed a hand along her arm. "Maybe in your shyness, you didn't realize someone had a crush on you."

"You're reaching. That's not it."

"Then what did you have in common with those girls? Or maybe—" he squirted a glob of ketchup on his plate "—the killer's after you because he thinks you saw something the night of Amanda's murder."

"That could be." Knitting her brows, Michelle stared out

the window. Tiffany, Amanda, Belinda, Jenny and Amy. Those girls had given her such a hard time in high school, with Amy as their ringleader.

Once they'd become friends as adults, Amanda had apologized for her treatment of Michelle. She'd tried to shrug off Amanda's mea culpa, but Amanda had been insistent about apologizing for one particular incident...an incident involving these five girls.

"What? Do you remember something?"

Michelle's sight focused on Colin across the table, dipping another fry into that puddle of ketchup. She crumpled the napkin in her lap and tossed it onto the plate with the half-eaten salad. "Yeah, I remember something."

Colin circled a fry in the air. "Well?"

"The year my mom took off with Eric, those girls played a prank. They spliced together my mom's picture with Eric's and submitted it to the yearbook for consideration for cutest couple." She dragged her fork through a dab of salad dressing on the table. "You know...those senior awards at the end of the year—best dressed, most athletic...you probably got that one."

He shrugged. "I did. Go on."

"There's not much more to it than that. They submitted the picture and got reprimanded by the principal."

"That doesn't seem so bad then if it never made it into the yearbook."

"Uh, well, it never made it into the yearbook, but it did make the rounds on campus. Just when I thought it was dying down. It seriously wrecked the end of my sophomore year."

Colin wiped his hands on his napkin and picked up the yearbook. "These five girls were involved in that prank?"

"Yep." She brushed her hands together. The memory of the prank hadn't stung quite as much as she'd expected it to. "So if anyone has a reason to murder those five girls, it's me."

"Maybe you're not a target, Michelle. If those girls pulled that joke on you, chances are they pulled more on other people. Maybe someone's really pissed off about one of those old pranks and decided to take revenge at the ten-year reunion."

"If I'm not a target for murder, why the camera? Why the vandalism to my car? Why lure me down to the supply closet? Why the failing brakes? Did I miss anything?"

"Peeping Tom."

"Thanks."

"Maybe the Reunion Killer wants an audience."

Hunching her shoulders, she hugged herself. "Why me?"

"I'm not sure." He scratched his chin, which he hadn't shaved since yesterday.

Michelle could still feel the scratchy roughness of it on the sensitive skin of her inner thighs. She blinked her eyes. How could she be sitting here daydreaming about making love with Colin when a killer had her in his sights…for whatever reason.

Colin smacked the book. "But this is a good start. There are lots of connections between the victims, and you may or may not be involved."

"I can ask some questions at the math faculty dinner tonight. Larry's wife was a teacher at the high school during that time, too."

"Did she quit?"

"Her heart wasn't in it, not like Larry's. And she didn't have to work—wealthy family. Her father's a judge in the next county."

"And, of course, Alec Wright was a student there, too."

She put one index finger over the other in a sign of the

cross. "I'm not going there, Colin. Alec has nothing to do with this."

Colin slid the check off the table. "I'll get this. Do you need to finish your grading at school, or can you do it at home?"

"I'm going to finish it at school." She held up a hand. "Don't worry. There are lots of teachers on campus finishing up, and we have a security guard wandering around."

"Keep your door locked and don't answer it for anyone, and I mean anyone."

"I promise. When I'm done, I'll see if Sue wants to go over to Larry's with me."

"I'll escort you home. What's his address?"

Michelle scribbled Larry's address on a scrap of paper from her purse and left it in the cup holder of Colin's new rental car, which had been delivered to his house this morning.

Colin drove her back to campus and gave her a quick kiss. "Be careful."

He waited at the curb until she got to the front door of the school, where a couple of teachers were taking a break on the steps.

She waved and slipped inside, touching her lips. That kiss had done more to make her feel safe than ten security guards.

Three hours later, Michelle hit the key for the final submission of her sixth-period grades. She checked the clock on the wall—half an hour until Larry's party.

Someone knocked on her classroom door, and she jumped. Her classroom was one of many on the second-story hallway. It had windows facing the street, but no view of the school corridor.

She crept to the door and placed her ear against it. "Who is it? Sue?"

Her breath rasped in her lungs and the blood pounded through her veins, sounding like a bass drum with her ear pressed against the door.

"Who is it?"

Hushed footsteps retreated.

Great.

She backed up to the desk, keeping an eye on the door. Holding her breath, she waited. Nothing.

She logged out of the grading website and shut down her laptop. She hitched her bag over her shoulder and killed the lights. Easing the door open, she peered into the empty hallway.

One of the classroom doors across from the staircase stood open, and she made a beeline for it. She ducked her head inside the room, startling one of the Spanish teachers bent over his desk.

Everyone was on edge.

"Sorry, Neil. Have you had your door open all afternoon?"

"Yeah."

"Someone knocked on my classroom door a little while ago. Did you see anyone coming down the hallway?"

He yawned and dropped his red pen. "No, but I've been grading these final projects for the past two hours, and I'm not sure I would've noticed a freight train barreling down the hallway."

"Okay. Maybe it was the security guard."

"Are you leaving? Do you want me to walk you to your car?"

"I'm going to stop by Sue Daniels's classroom. We're going to Larry's get-together tonight."

Neil rolled his eyes. "You math geeks really know how to party down, don't you?"

She laughed and left him to his grading. Glancing back

at Neil's classroom, she turned the corner to Sue's room. At least Neil was within screaming distance.

Knocking on Sue's door, she called out, "Are you done? Ready to go to Larry's?"

Sue didn't answer, so Michelle tried the door handle. It was locked. She knocked again. "Sue?"

A chill crept up her spine like a cold finger, and she backed away from the door. She returned to Neil's room. "I'll take you up on your offer to walk me out to my car. Did you happen to see Sue leave?"

Neil tapped his papers before pushing to his feet. "Buried in *español*."

By the time Michelle reached the Brunswicks' house, her shoulders ached and her eyes burned from tension. On the drive over, her gaze had been bouncing between the road in front of her and the road behind her in the rearview mirror. She wanted to make sure nobody was following her from the high school.

The way the fog was rolling in again, she could be lost in a cocoon of gray mist, silenced, cut off from everyone except a killer. She shivered. Had Amanda experienced that or had she never seen it coming?

Michelle didn't have that luxury. She knew something was coming, she just didn't know when or from what direction. The menace of the day had soaked into her bones, permeated the cells of her flesh.

The lights burning from almost every window in the Brunswick house warmed her, welcomed her, and she let out a long breath when she reached the door.

Larry opened the door, and his eyes popped wide. "You're early."

"I am? Six-thirty?"

"Actually, it's six-twenty, and the party's at seven." He gestured her in with one arm. "Enter. Nancy's in the shower.

Can I get you something to drink? Soda? Hot tea? Iced tea? I know you don't drink wine."

Michelle took a turn around the room. "Iced tea is fine."

For once she wished she weren't a teetotaler. She could use a drink...or two, because the tension that gripped her in a vise had followed her right into Larry's house.

AFTER A FRUITLESS AFTERNOON at the police station, Colin had retreated to Burgers and Brews to shoot some pool, eat a real burger and down a couple of beers.

The beers hadn't done a thing to loosen the tightness of his gut. Everything felt wrong today. The marine layer that had crawled onto shore, blanketing everything in a murky haze, added to the sense of doom that hung over Coral Cove.

He checked his watch—almost seven. Michelle would be at her party, and he had a couple of hours to kill before escorting her home.

Colin wandered out of his friend's establishment and balanced on the curb, his hands shoved in his pockets. The whoosh of wheels and the creaking of a bicycle chain cut through the fog, and Colin recognized Alec Wright pedaling away on his bike.

Must've just finished up at the high school and was on his way to the math shindig. Colin didn't like the idea of that dude in the same room as Michelle.

Colin glanced in the direction of the high school. The school would still be open, unlocked for those teachers working on grades, and it looked like the graduation rehearsal was going on.

His steps carried him to the football field where the members of the graduating class were forming lines, walking across a stage and generally screwing around. Nothing changed.

He strode into the main building like he belonged there

and took the familiar path to the front office. Mrs. Seville was still working, same glasses perched on the end of her nose.

He leaned into the office. "Hello, Mrs. Seville."

She looked up from her computer with a scowl, which melted in an instant. "Hello, Colin. I heard you were back in town. Not very good timing."

"Are you safe in here working on your own?"

"I have those security guards trained to come by here every ten minutes. Besides I have teachers coming in out and—" she swiveled her head from side to side and whispered "—I graduated a lot longer than ten years ago."

"Be careful." Then he put on his best football hero smile. "I need to get into Alec Wright's classroom. Ms. Girard, the math teacher, left something in there and asked me to pick it up for her since they're both at a faculty event."

"Must be Larry's get-together. I'm surprised he's having it this year." She shook her finger at Colin. "I heard you were spending some time with Michelle Girard. Don't charm her and then break her heart. She's a good girl."

He had every intention of charming Michelle. The broken heart? That just might be his. "Michelle's one in a million."

She reached into a drawer and pulled out a key chain. "Here's the master. Make sure you return it when you're done or the principal will have my head. I'm getting ready to wrap up, so slip it under the office door. I'll be back in tomorrow."

Colin swept the key from the counter and blew out the breath he'd been holding. Mrs. Seville had always had a soft spot for jocks. "Thanks, Mrs. S. I'll get it back to you. Oh, and where's his classroom?"

"JR 202. Do you remember? It's the next building over next to the auditorium."

Colin did remember and jogged out of the main building into the quad before Mrs. S had second thoughts.

Luckily, the band was practicing in the auditorium, so the security guards wouldn't question Colin's presence in this building. He located 202 and slipped the key into the lock, shoving the door open with his hip.

The lights were still on, so maybe the custodian hadn't hit this room yet. Colin didn't know what he hoped to find. A bloody knife?

The desk drawers were unlocked. He rifled through them, discovering nothing more than printed assignments, lesson plans and a few school supplies. The guy didn't keep anything personal here. Colin would like a crack at Alec's house.

He checked his watch. The party must be in full swing.

He locked the door of the computer lab behind him and stopped at the entrance to the auditorium to listen to the band practice. Folding his arms, he wedged his shoulder against an open doorway.

After a loud crescendo where the drums reverberated in his chest, the conductor took it down several notches and the light sounds of the flutes trilled across the auditorium. *Not bad.*

Another sound intruded on the dulcet tones of the flutes. Colin tilted his head and held his breath. A soft sob came out of the darkness of the room behind him.

He whispered. "Hello?"

The sobbing stopped, replaced by snuffling and sniffing. Reminded him of the time he'd stumbled on Michelle crying at the beach.

"Are you okay?" His eyes adjusted to the dark, and he saw a form huddled among the broken music stands and old instrument cases. "Come on out."

"Mr. Roarke?" A pair of wide eyes gleamed at him from the gloom.

"Maddie?" This girl was doing a lot of hiding out and crying. "What are you doing in here? Nick's already out of the hospital, right? He's doing okay."

She scuffled to her feet and weaved toward him, rubbing her eyes. "He's okay."

"Then what's wrong?" Maybe he'd missed his calling. He should've been a high school counselor.

She dropped her chin to her chest, and her long hair fell over her face. "I-is Ms. Girard going to tell on Nick?"

"For what, Maddie?" Colin's fingers curled around a seat back, digging into the cushion.

"You know…for sending those emails."

A muscle ticked in Colin's jaw, but he measured his words. "What do you know about those emails?"

Still not showing her face, Maddie picked at her fingernail. "It wasn't Nick's fault. He caught Nick cheating and threatened to tell on him. He made Nick send those emails. A-and he does things with the girls, Mr. Roarke."

Colin's blood started to percolate. "What kinds of things, Maddie?"

"He touches my knee sometimes, and when girls are wearing low-cut blouses, he makes them sit in the front of the room." She crossed her arms over her chest. "It's creepy."

"Have you ever thought of reporting him?"

"Oh, no." Shaking her head, she shoved her hair back from her face. "He finds out stuff about us, and he's too important. He's been around a long time."

As the bile churned in his gut, Colin narrowed his eyes. "Mr. Wright hasn't been around that long."

"Mr. Wright?" Maddie threw a quick glance at the stage where the band was wrapping up. "I'm not talking about Mr. Wright. He's cool."

"Who are you talking about?"

"Mr. Brunswick."

Colin's heart thudded in his chest with thick dread. "Mr. Brunswick made Nick send those emails? He's the one who's been inappropriate with the girls?"

"Yes." She licked her lips and kicked the bottom of the chair with the toe of her high-tops. "He thinks he's all in shape because he pumps iron, but he's just gross...and weird."

Brunswick—and Michelle was at his house for a party. He'd have to play it cool when he picked her up, even though he wanted to smash his fist into the man's face. He needed something more than an unstable schoolgirl's tales.

Colin fingered the master key in his pocket. "Where's his room, Maddie? Where's Mr. Brunswick's classroom?"

"It's in the main building...where Ms. Procter was murdered." She hugged herself around the middle. "Y-you don't think Mr. Brunswick had anything to do with that, do you?"

"Do you? Is that why you've been upset? You wouldn't want Nick involved in murder."

Fresh tears welled up in the girl's eyes and spilled over onto her cheeks. "He's not messed up in anything like that, Mr. Roarke. Mr. Brunswick caught Nick getting some answers to one of Ms. Girard's quizzes from another student and made him send those emails. That's all."

"Do you think Mr. Brunswick had anything to do with Nick's accident?"

Maddie pinned him with a wide, glassy gaze. "Yes."

"What's Mr. Brunswick's room number?"

"It's 226."

He took Maddie by the shoulders and spun her around. "Get home."

She called after his retreating back. "Are you going to help Nick?"

"I'm going to help everyone." Could he really do it this time?

Colin charged across the quad and pushed through the

doors of the main building. The custodian hadn't locked up yet. He took the steps two at a time, passing Michelle's classroom on the way to 226.

He slid the master key into the lock on Brunswick's door and slipped inside the room, flicking on the lights. He headed for the desk and tried the top drawer. Locked. Brunswick obviously had more to protect than Wright did.

He withdrew a switchblade from his pocket and jimmied the lock. Bingo. The lock popped and Colin slid open the drawer.

He shuffled through the stuff in the top drawer—same junk as Wright's drawer. He yanked open the second drawer and thumbed through lesson plans and answer sheets.

The larger bottom drawer squeaked when he pulled it open. A stack of papers almost reached the top of the drawer. Colin licked the pads of his thumb and index finger and began lifting each piece of paper.

Did the guy throw anything away? Dog-eared tests, old Scantrons and notes sifted through his fingers.

He scanned one of the old tests from a bygone student and glanced at the name at the top of the paper. He froze as his blood turned to ice water in his veins.

Michelle Girard.

He turned over the page for the next test. This one belonged to Michelle also…and the next and the next. It looked like Brunswick had saved every honors algebra two test Michelle had ever taken. That was just weird.

He reached the bottom of the drawer and froze. His fingers skimmed over the picture of Michelle, topless, in her panties and in her bedroom. It was a still from a video.

Adrenaline pushed through his system and he slammed his fist on top of the desk. It had been Brunswick—the emails, the camera…probably the murders.

Michelle hadn't been a target. Brunswick had been avenging her. He had some strange obsession with her and was wreaking vengeance on her supposed enemies. Until she'd joined forces with Colin...then Brunswick's wrath had turned against her.

Colin clutched the picture and all the papers to his chest and slammed the drawer shut. He stormed out of the room and ran down the steps to the front office. He slid the master key under the door and headed for the exit.

He almost collided with a woman flying through the doors.

"My God. You scared me." She clutched her hands to her chest. "Oh, hello, handsome."

It was the geometry teacher from Michelle's classroom earlier today. His heart banged against his ribs. He forced the words out of his raw throat. "Aren't you supposed to be at Brunswick's party?"

Her dark brows shot up. "There's no party tonight, is there?"

"What do you mean? Michelle went to the party." Pain stabbed his temple and he squinted his eye against it.

"I guess Michelle didn't get the memo. Larry canceled that party."

Chapter Fifteen

Michelle took the glass with tinkling ice from Larry's hand. She downed half the liquid before Larry even took a sip from his drink. "I just came from grading. I'm so thirsty."

"Let me pour you a little more." He retreated to the kitchen and returned with a topped-off glass.

"Thanks, Larry." She sipped the tea more slowly this time. "Nancy's still in the shower?"

"I'll tell her the guests are beginning to arrive."

He made for the staircase, and Michelle's gaze wandered to the front door. The guests *weren't* beginning to arrive. Where was the food? The music? Larry's wife prided herself on throwing a good party.

Nobody had been in the mood for a party. Maybe they should've canceled this year.

She rose from the sofa and trailed her hand along the mantel above the marble fireplace. Pictures of Larry and Nancy, and Nancy and her father smiled back at her. The Brunswicks had never had kids—strange, considering they were both teachers. Larry had always had his favorite students as substitute children, though. She'd been his teacher's pet for sure.

Larry glided down the stairs. "She's almost ready. Sends her apologies. Nobody else here yet?"

"No. Seems like a low-key party this time around."

"Well, under the circumstances…" He fluffed a cushion on the back of the couch. "Have a seat. I'll get some food."

Some food? Nancy usually had trays of hot hors d'oeuvres scattered around the room. Michelle's stomach rumbled. She hadn't eaten since lunch with Colin and she'd barely touched her salad.

She rolled her wrist to see her watch. After seven now. She just wanted Colin to pick her up and take her home.

Larry returned from the kitchen bearing a cutting board layered with chunks of cheese and crackers. Wow, Nancy had really lowered her standards.

He set it down on the coffee table in front of her. "Just until Nancy gets down here and puts the finishing touches on the rest of the hors d'oeuvres."

Michelle's gaze traveled up the silent staircase. Nancy had been awfully quiet up there. A whisper of apprehension brushed her skin.

"Larry, maybe it wasn't a great idea to have the party this year." She waved her hand at the door. "It doesn't look like anyone else is going to show up."

Larry roamed to the window with his hands in his pockets. "Nobody called to cancel. At least have some cheese and crackers, Michelle. You must be hungry after grading all afternoon."

Her stomach rolled again, so she reached for a cracker. It took her three tries to shove a piece of cheese onto the little square. She flexed her fingers before picking it up and taking a bite.

Her hand fell to her lap and the cheese tumbled to the floor. "I'm sorry."

She made an effort to lift her hand from her lap to retrieve the cheese, but it proved too much and she sank back into the cushion.

"Are you tired, Michelle?"

"So tired. Lethargic." Her brain seemed to be functioning fine, but her limbs felt like lead. She must be ill. "Larry, I need to go home."

The cushion on the couch dipped as he sat beside her. "You're not going to your home, Michelle. You're coming to a new home with me."

Her hand jerked in response to her brain's command. "What are you talking about?"

He took one of her hands between his, and even though her brain screamed at her muscles to move, they wouldn't budge.

"I've waited a long time for this, Michelle. I figured ten years was just the right amount of time. You're a grown woman now. At your age, you wouldn't feel as if I were robbing the cradle, like your mother did with Eric."

"My mother?"

"She was a slut, but you're different, Michelle." He squeezed her hand. "I did have to remind you now and then. You'd gone out with Alec a few too many times and then Colin Roarke, the football hero showed up."

"Colin." She wanted to scream his name but her vocal cords wouldn't cooperate. Where was he? When would he come for her?

"He's not your type, Michelle. You belong with me."

"Where's your wife?" Michelle dragged her gaze up the staircase again to the empty hallway. She knew Nancy wasn't here.

"Nancy." He snapped his fingers. "She's on some jaunt with her father. She got scared after the second murder."

"Did you, did you...?"

"Of course I killed those girls. They tortured you in high school. Blamed you for your mother's actions. I had to tie up everything with a nice ribbon for you. How could I ever ask you for your hand in marriage without taking care of business first?"

"Marriage?" She shuffled her feet. "Larry, let me go home. I promise I won't tell anyone."

He shook a finger in her face. "Don't get me mad, Michelle. Of course you'll tell. You actually befriended that Amanda, and now you're friendly with Colin the FBI agent."

Larry's face reddened and he tossed her hand away from him. "I saw you with him. That's why I had to put that reminder on your car. And then Maddie told me you were with him again."

"You used Maddie?"

"Stupid slut. I caught her and her cheater boyfriend, Nick Schaeffer, making out at Columbella House, defiling it. I threatened to tell her mother unless she agreed to help me out."

Michelle's stomach rolled again, with nausea this time.

"Don't worry, Michelle. I forgive you everything. I'm actually glad Roarke's car didn't go off the side of a cliff. That's why I sent Maddie to check up on you." He pushed to his feet and opened the front door. "It's time to go."

Michelle clenched her muscles, but she couldn't make them act. "Where are we going, Larry?"

"We're going to consummate our love, because I know you love me, too, Michelle. You turned to me when you were a teen—so fresh and lovely—so different from those sluts."

"What sluts, Larry? The girls you murdered?"

He wedged his arms beneath her limp body and hoisted her over his shoulder. He marched toward the open front door and carried her into the misty night.

Oh, God. He was taking her somewhere else. How would Colin ever find her now?

As Larry turned to lock the door, Michelle asked in a muffled voice, "Where are we going, Larry?"

"To consummate our love…at Columbella House."

How was Colin going to find her at Columbella? It was close to his own house, so maybe he'd see a light again. But what were the chances of that?

Larry wedged himself between his car and hers parked next to it in the driveway. The Brunswicks had no neighbors nearby. There was nobody on the street, and even if there were somebody out there, Larry's driveway was set back. Nobody would notice a man carrying a woman over his shoulder.

Once he got her in his car and into Columbella House, it would be all over for her. Would Colin notice the car on the street? Would someone on the block see them enter the house? The Vincents were still on vacation.

She couldn't leave it to chance.

When Larry reached for the car door handle, a surge of adrenaline fueled by fear poured through Michelle's body. She gritted her teeth and focused every bit of her concentration on her right hand, dangling in the air.

She lifted her hand. She stiffened her fingers. She reached for her car window already coated with condensation from the low clouds. She plowed her fingers into the moist chalkboard and managed to eke out two letters: *CH.*

Larry swung the back door open so hard, it banged the side of Michelle's car. "Oops, sorry."

He ducked, taking her with him, and then gently laid her across his backseat. After tucking her legs in after her, Larry slammed the door shut.

His shoes crunched the gravel of his long driveway and then he slid into the driver's seat and cranked on the engine. "That was surprisingly easy. Who says you never use math again after high school? I planned out every detail of our honeymoon like a mathematical equation."

Michelle squeezed her eyes shut and prayed hard. *Please find me, Colin. Rescue me from this madman.*

NO PARTY. NO PARTY. Michelle had gone to the Brunswicks' house on her own. Did she have any idea the man had a crazy crush on her? No, she didn't know.

The insidious fog had rolled in early and heavy. Colin wanted to speed down the street to rescue Michelle from that so-called party, but he had to take it slow and easy. The muscles in his leg ached as he held off on slamming down the accelerator.

He navigated the streets of downtown Coral Cove and then hit the highway toward Brunswick's address. He did not live in one of the developed housing tracts. His house was one of a few sprinkled along the low-lying hills that ran down to the highway bordering the coastline.

He turned up Brunswick's street with dread thumping in his chest. No streetlights. Houses set far apart and recessed. Quiet.

He peered into the darkness to read the iridescent numbers on the mailboxes and finally located Brunswick's—a house set far back from the road. He drove up the long driveway churning up gravel.

One vehicle stood sentry in front of a two-car garage… Michelle's car. The sight of that little Honda eased the tension in his shoulders, and he loosened his grip on the steering wheel for the first time since he'd gotten in the car.

She'd have to know by now something was wrong. *Hold on, Michelle.*

Colin rang the doorbell like a civilized caller even though he wanted to burst through the door and carry Michelle away over his shoulder. He knocked. He tried to peek through the heavy curtains pulled across the front windows.

He banged on the door, his fists pummeling the thick slab of wood. Where were they? Where was Michelle?

With the butt of his gun, he broke the front window. Reaching through the jagged glass, he unlocked the latch and slid open the window.

He climbed through and landed on the hardwood floor of the dining room. He leveled his weapon in front of him. "Hello?"

He crept into the next room, the kitchen. There had been no attempt to even make it look as if there was going to be a party. From the kitchen, he entered the living room, gun first.

A full tray of cheese and crackers sat on the coffee table alongside a glass of mostly melted ice cubes. Colin picked up the glass with two fingers and sniffed the contents. His nostrils flared. The liquid had a funny smell. Had Brunswick drugged Michelle?

His rage blinded him, and he swept the tray of food from the table. With fists clenched he circled the room. He must've taken her somewhere else. What had he done with his wife?

Colin charged up the stairs, throwing open the doors to every room. Nothing. Nobody.

He jogged back down the stairs and found the door to the attached garage. A gleaming Mercedes sat on one side of the two-car garage, and the other spot was empty.

He'd taken her. Brunswick had drugged Michelle and taken her somewhere.

The ice in her glass wasn't completely melted, and she'd just gotten here around six-thirty. They couldn't be far. He'd track them down. He'd call the police.

He left through the front door, leaving it ajar, and stalked into the driveway where he'd parked behind Michelle's car. As he passed her car, he flipped up the door handle. The beaded moisture on the outside of her window was dripping. Still gripping the handle, he leaned back. He caught his breath when he noticed writing in the condensation.

Two letters: *CH*. Michelle had sent him a signal, and he had no doubt about its meaning.

Brunswick had taken her to Columbella House.

MICHELLE WIGGLED HER TOES as she reclined on the high four-poster bed with the flowered bedspread. To get to this room, Larry had released a secret panel in the library. The room was better preserved than the rest of the house, or at least cleaner. Larry must've been using it for a while now.

He busied himself lighting scented candles around the room. "I want this to be perfect, Michelle, perfect for our first time."

"Why here, Larry? Why this house and why this room?" The longer she could keep him talking, the more time Colin had to reach her. She had confidence in Colin. He had good tracking skills. Surely he'd notice the disturbance in the dust patterns. And if he didn't, she'd make sure he found her another way.

Larry cocked his head. "I love this house, Michelle. It could've been mine, you know. I'm a member of the St. Regis family. My great-grandmother was the sister of the original St. Regis who built this house. If he hadn't had children, he would've left the house to his sister, my great-grandmother. I never would've let it fall into disrepair like those two St. Regis twins. If Marissa St. Regis hadn't been a slut and run off with Mia's boyfriend, it would be different now."

"H-how did you know about this room?"

"I played here as a child. This house is a child's paradise—all kinds of secret nooks."

And Larry seemed to know all of them. He'd parked his

car off the highway and taken a route along the coast to come in through the basement, a scary, creepy place that had given Michelle goose bumps.

That's probably how he had gotten away after killing Amanda.

"Are you regaining some feeling in your limbs, Michelle?" He turned toward a cherry armoire and opened it. He pulled out a white, lacey dress. "Your wedding dress."

Michelle's body shook with revulsion, and her hands convulsively grasped the bedspread.

"I want to do this right. I want us to say our vows before our consummation." He tossed the dress across her body.

The sweet smell of camphor filled her nostrils, and she turned her head away from the lace scratching her chin.

"Ah, very good. You can move. I don't want you to be completely paralyzed during our honeymoon." He opened a drawer and withdrew a long, gleaming knife. "But I do need your cooperation."

Her legs jerked as another wave of adrenaline coursed through her veins. Did he plan to kill her after he raped her? What else? What else could he do with her? He couldn't stash her away in this room forever like some forgotten bride.

"I'm going to help you into the dress. I'll try not to peek, but really, Michelle, it's not like I haven't seen it all before…seen you all before." He shook his finger in her face. "Naughty girl, undressing for the camera."

Sour bile rose from her gut and she swallowed hard.

Larry removed her shoes and unbuttoned her skirt. He yanked it down over her hips. The moist, dank air crept around her bare legs and she shivered.

"I know it's chilly in here, but soon you'll be in your beautiful wedding dress. See if you can lift your arms."

Michelle raised her arms with relief. At least the effects

of whatever drug he gave her were wearing off. She could fight back.

She watched the corded muscles of his arms as he pulled the sweater over her head and her pulse skittered. Larry had been working out, buffing up. The math teacher was in good shape.

"You can leave your brassiere on for this dress. This is no wedding dress for a slut."

There was that word again. Who knew Larry Brunswick was so obsessed with sluts? Who knew Larry Brunswick was a killer?

Larry held out the dress for her, and she was able to swing her legs from the bed. She didn't have the energy to attack him now, but she was storing it up…and then all hell would break loose.

He dropped to his knees before her and held open the dress. Michelle stepped into it with heavy legs. Larry helped her to her feet where she swayed. He caught her around the waist and sniffed her neck.

Michelle gagged.

He pulled the dress up and around her and she stuck her arms through the tight, lace sleeves, which he buttoned at her wrists. With his hands on her bare shoulders, he turned her around, pulled the bodice of the dress tight, and began fastening the small buttons at the back.

His fingertips on her skin made her feel dirty and sick.

He spun her around again, his dark eyes shining with a crazy, frantic glow. "You don't know how long I've dreamed of this, Michelle. You and I together. I'm your conquering hero. I vanquished all your enemies to be with you. Say it, Michelle."

"I—I, what do you want me to say, Larry?"

He pinched her chin between his thumb and forefinger,

his eyes stormy. "Say I'm you're conquering hero—your one and only."

He reached behind him for the knife, and Michelle swallowed. "You're my conquering hero, Larry. My one and only."

He smiled and planted a kiss on her unresponsive lips. "I wrote my own wedding vows."

He dragged her in front of a full-length mirror. Her reflection stared back at her like the bride of Frankenstein. The dress had been designed for a much shorter and plumper woman. The lace and satin sagged and puckered around her torso and the hem hit her midshin. Above the dress, her white face was smeared with makeup and her disheveled hair fell around her shoulders in a tangle.

Larry solemnly took both of her hands. He recited a speech, half love poem and half angry diatribe against her enemies. When he finished, he placed a heavy ring on her left hand, an heirloom of some kind.

"I know you haven't had time to write your vows, Michelle. All I ask is that you repeat what you said before. I will die a happy man."

Die? Did Larry plan to die?

Michelle licked her lips, gaining more control over her body with every minute. "You're my conquering hero. My one and only."

Larry gave a whoop like he was at a football game and pulled her into his arms, crushing her against his chest. "I knew it. I knew you loved me."

He held her away from him, raking her body with his hungry gaze. "I want to consummate our marriage with you wearing your wedding dress, Michelle. You never looked more beautiful than at this moment."

Holding her, he walked her back to the bed. At that

moment, a thump resounded from the room beyond the panel. Larry froze.

Michelle's heart jumped. Could it be Colin? Did he find and understand her message?

Larry shrugged. "Probably more of those stupid kids making out. They'll never hear us in this room."

Was it true? How could the room be soundproof? She didn't see any evidence of it.

She pulled in a long breath and let loose with a scream.

The smack came quick and hard. Her cheek stung and her eyes watered.

Larry shoved her back onto the bed, his eyes blazing. "Slut. Keep your mouth shut."

He didn't have his knife and he probably really wanted to consummate this mock marriage, so she screamed again.

This time he punched her in the gut. As she gasped for breath he reached behind him and grabbed the knife. "If you scream again, I'll slice you."

She choked. "I'm sorry, Larry. You're my conquering hero. My one and only."

The words worked like a magic charm. He placed the knife on the nightstand, next to a flickering candle and smoothed his palm across her burning cheek. "That's better. Don't be afraid. I won't make love to you like I did with those sluts. And I know you won't make love like they did, either."

Michelle's heart hammered. Which sluts was he talking about now? Not his students. Please, God, not his female students.

He swept the knife from the nightstand and dropped it to the floor. The gesture caused the candle holder to wobble, the flame dancing too close to the bed canopy.

Fully clothed, he fell on top of her, burying his face in

her neck. She twisted her head to the side. Had Colin heard her screams?

The candle was still wobbling. She had to make a move… now. She coiled her muscles and focused. Her hand shot out, knocking the candle toward the swaying fringe on the canopy. Wisps of smoke rose from the fringe, and then a small ember flared to life.

Larry thought she'd hit her hand on the headboard. He grabbed her fingers and brought them to his lips. "Be careful. The drug will wear off soon."

His trembling hands bunched in the satin skirt of the dress. "It's time, Michelle."

It's time, all right.

He sat up, his eyes glazed over with lust. As he reached for the fly of his pants, Michelle heaved her body to the side and rolled from the bed. She grabbed the kindling canopy on her way down.

Larry yelled and rolled off the other side of the bed. "What are you doing?"

She tossed the canopy at the bedspread, where it ignited.

Larry glared at her through the flames. "You think a little fire is going to stop me?"

The room began filling with smoke and Michelle coughed. Someone started banging on the wall. She screamed. "Colin! Colin!"

Larry crawled on the floor to the other side of the burning bed. He grabbed her ankle as she started moving toward the panel.

"You're not getting out of here. We have to consummate our marriage." He started dragging her backward toward the flames as her fingernails scraped against the floor.

She scrabbled to find traction, something to keep her from being pulled back into Larry Brunswick's insane world and the flames engulfing the bed.

The sound of gunshots and then splintering wood rose above the crackle of the fire. Larry's grip tightened. Michelle tried to kick him with her other foot, but he cinched that ankle in a vise.

Colin crashed through the panel, his gun pointing at Larry. "Let her go or I'll shoot you right where you are."

Larry released his grip and then flung himself on top of the flaming bed. His screams filled the room and Michelle covered her ears.

Colin swept her up in his arms and carried her out of the burning room and then outside into the moist sea air. He sank into the sand at the side of Columbella House and cupped her face with his strong, sure hands. "I've got you. I've got you now, and I'm never letting you go."

Sobbing, she hugged him around the neck. She had a hero, and his name was Colin Roarke.

Epilogue

Michelle clung to Colin's hand as they stood inside her yard chatting to Lieutenant Trammell. The sun had burst through at ten o'clock this morning—had to be a record for this week.

Lieutenant Trammell was shaking his head. "Yeah, if we'd had Brunswick's DNA, we could've wrapped this up a lot sooner."

"You should've told me you guys had collected a hair sample from both crime scenes. I could've suggested a few suspects to check out." Colin pulled her closer until they were shoulder to shoulder.

"We should've listened to you earlier about those two other murders, Roarke."

Michelle squeezed Colin's hand. "I can't believe Larry had been in trouble with prostitutes before, beating them. Any whiff of a scandal like that and he'd have lost his teaching job."

"That's why his father-in-law, the judge, covered it up for him, made it go away." Trammell rolled his eyes. "Friends in high places."

"And Nick's okay?"

"The boy's spooked but fine. He didn't realize Brunswick was the killer, but when Brunswick ran him off the road that day, he was afraid to cross him."

A tremble rolled through Michelle's body and Colin

wrapped an arm around her. He pointed to Columbella House. "How badly did the fire damage it?"

"It's not as bad as it could've been. That room contained most of it, including Brunswick's crispy body."

Michelle turned her head into Colin's shoulder.

"Mia St. Regis is going to have to come back and do something about the house or the city's going to condemn it."

"Thanks for the update, Lieutenant." Colin stuck out his hand, and it was a dismissal.

They shook hands and Lieutenant Trammell sauntered back to his car.

"Cops need to be more careful in the way they talk about crime scenes to civilians." He rubbed her back and kissed the side of her head.

"I don't think I'm ever going to get the sound of Larry's scream out of my head."

"We'll just have to fill it with more pleasant sounds." He tapped her temple.

"So when are you going back to work?" Michelle held her breath. They'd already agreed to a long-distance relationship until they could work out the details of their work situations, but Michelle couldn't bear to be apart from him so soon.

"You mean I didn't tell you?"

The breath puffed from her lips and she slugged his shoulder. "No."

He laughed. "I'm extending my vacation to coincide with yours. My boss was damned grateful I solved those two other murders. He would've handed me anything…but all I want is more time with you."

"That's great." She hugged him and kissed his mouth. She'd been initiating kisses a lot lately. "Where are we going?"

"Someplace warm and tropical where the sun shines all day long."

"Hawaii?"

"Let's do it."

Hand in hand they turned toward Michelle's house. She stuck her other hand in the pocket of her shorts and felt the bracelet. She pulled it out and dangled it in front of her where it caught the sunlight and winked back at her.

"Look. It's the bracelet you found in the basement at Columbella House. It belongs to Marissa or Mia. If it's Mia's, I wonder if she wants it back."

"And if she doesn't?"

Michelle turned and stared at the house across the street. Even with the sun glinting off the leaded windows and a profusion of scarlet bougainvillea creeping along the trellises, Columbella House exuded a dark aura. It glared back at her.

She shivered and turned away. Tossing the bracelet into the air, she said, "Maybe I'll keep it. After all, my mom made it."

Colin kissed her, long and hard. "You've come a long way, Michelle Girard."

She *had* come a long way from that shy schoolgirl, and she owed it all to her hometown hero.

* * * * *

SUSPENSE

Harlequin®

INTRIGUE®

REQUEST YOUR FREE BOOKS!
2 FREE NOVELS PLUS 2 FREE GIFTS!

Harlequin®

INTRIGUE®

BREATHTAKING ROMANTIC SUSPENSE

YES! Please send me 2 FREE Harlequin Intrigue® novels and my 2 FREE gifts (gifts are worth about $10). After receiving them, if I don't wish to receive any more books, I can return the shipping statement marked "cancel." If I don't cancel, I will receive 6 brand-new novels every month and be billed just $4.49 per book in the U.S. or $5.24 per book in Canada. That's a saving of at least 14% off the cover price! It's quite a bargain! Shipping and handling is just 50¢ per book in the U.S. and 75¢ per book in Canada.* I understand that accepting the 2 free books and gifts places me under no obligation to buy anything. I can always return a shipment and cancel at any time. Even if I never buy another book, the two free books and gifts are mine to keep forever.

182/382 HDN FEQ2

Name	(PLEASE PRINT)	
Address		Apt. #
City	State/Prov.	Zip/Postal Code

Signature (if under 18, a parent or guardian must sign)

Mail to the **Reader Service:**
IN U.S.A.: P.O. Box 1867, Buffalo, NY 14240-1867
IN CANADA: P.O. Box 609, Fort Erie, Ontario L2A 5X3

Not valid for current subscribers to Harlequin Intrigue books.

**Are you a subscriber to Harlequin Intrigue books
and want to receive the larger-print edition?
Call 1-800-873-8635 or visit www.ReaderService.com.**

* Terms and prices subject to change without notice. Prices do not include applicable taxes. Sales tax applicable in N.Y. Canadian residents will be charged applicable taxes. Offer not valid in Quebec. This offer is limited to one order per household. All orders subject to credit approval. Credit or debit balances in a customer's account(s) may be offset by any other outstanding balance owed by or to the customer. Please allow 4 to 6 weeks for delivery. Offer available while quantities last.

Your Privacy—The Reader Service is committed to protecting your privacy. Our Privacy Policy is available online at www.ReaderService.com or upon request from the Reader Service.

We make a portion of our mailing list available to reputable third parties that offer products we believe may interest you. If you prefer that we not exchange your name with third parties, or if you wish to clarify or modify your communication preferences, please visit us at www.ReaderService.com/consumerschoice or write to us at Reader Service Preference Service, P.O. Box 9062, Buffalo, NY 14269. Include your complete name and address.

HI11B

Harlequin® Romantic Suspense presents the final book in the gripping **PERFECT, WYOMING** *miniseries from best-loved veteran series author Carla Cassidy*

Witness as mercenary Micah Grayson and cult escapee Olivia Conner join forces to save a little boy and to take down a monster, while desire explodes between them....

Read on for an excerpt from
MERCENARY'S PERFECT MISSION

Available June 2012 from Harlequin® Romantic Suspense.

"**I** won't tell," she exclaimed fervently. "Please don't hurt me. I swear I won't tell anyone what I saw. Just let me have my other son and we'll go far away from here. I'll never speak your name again." Her voice cracked as she focused on his gun and he realized she believed he was Samuel.

Certainly it was dark enough that it would be easy for anyone to mistake him for his brother. When the brothers were together it was easy to see the subtle differences between them. Micah's face was slightly thinner, his features more chiseled than those of his brother.

At the moment Micah knew Samuel kept his hair cut neat and tidy, while Micah's long hair was tied back. He reached up and pulled the rawhide strip, allowing his hair to fall from its binding.

The woman gasped once again. "You aren't him...but you look like him. Who are you?" Her voice still held fear as she dropped the stick and protectively clutched the baby closer to her chest.

"Who are you?" he countered. He wasn't about to be taken in by a pale-haired angel with big green eyes in this evil place where angels probably couldn't exist.

"I'm Olivia Conner, and this is my son Sam." Tears filled her eyes. "I have another son, but he's still in town. I couldn't get to him before I ran away. I've heard rumors that there was a safe house somewhere, but I've been in the woods for two days and I can't find it."

Micah was unmoved by her tears and by her story. He knew how devious his brother could be, and Micah would do everything possible to protect the location of the safe house. There was only one way to know for sure if she was one of Samuel's "devotees."

Will Olivia be able to get her son back from the clutches of evil? Or will Micah's maniacal twin put an end to them all? Find out in the shocking conclusion to the PERFECT, WYOMING *miniseries.*

MERCENARY'S PERFECT MISSION
Available June 2012, only from
Harlequin® Romantic Suspense, wherever books are sold.

HRSEXP0612

SPECIAL EDITION

Life, Love and Family

USA TODAY bestselling author

Marie Ferrarella

enchants readers in

ONCE UPON A MATCHMAKER

Micah Muldare's aunt is worried that her nephew is going to wind up alone in his old age...but this matchmaking mama has just the thing! When Micah finds himself accused of theft, defense lawyer Tracy Ryan agrees to help him as a favor to his aunt, but soon finds herself drawn to more than just his case. Will Micah open up his heart and realize Tracy is his match?

Available June 2012

Saddle up with Harlequin® series books this summer and find a cowboy for every mood!

Available wherever books are sold.

www.Harlequin.com

HSE65674

Fall under the spell of fan-favorite author

Leslie Kelly

Workaholic Mimi Burdette thinks she's satisfied dating the handsome man her father has picked out for her. But when sexy firefighter Xander McKinley moves into her apartment building, Mimi finds herself becoming…distracted. When Mimi opens a fortune cookie predicting who will be the man of her dreams, then starts having erotic dreams, she never imagines Xander is having the same dreams! Until they come together and bring those dreams to life.

Blazing Midsummer Nights

The magic begins June 2012

Saddle up with Harlequin® series books this summer and find a cowboy for every mood!

Available wherever books are sold.

Harlequin *Romance*

A touching new duet from fan-favorite author

SUSAN MEIER

First Time
DADS!

When millionaire CEO Max Montgomery spots
Kate Hunter-Montgomery—the wife he's never forgotten—
back in town with a daughter who looks just like him, he's
determined to win her back. But can this savvy business tycoon
convince Kate to trust him a second time with her heart?

Find out this June in

THE TYCOON'S SECRET DAUGHTER

And look for book 2 coming this August!

NANNY FOR THE MILLIONAIRE'S TWINS

Saddle up with Harlequin® series books this summer
and find a cowboy for every mood!